I0689736

Unexpected Attachments: A Queer Circus Romance

Cirque Callisto Series Book Two

Madison Nicole

MN Books LLC

PREFACE

Unexpected Attachments is the second book in the Cirque Callisto Series, a four-book series of interconnected standalones. Each book can be read on its own but is best read in numerical order. If you haven't read *Tangled Encounters*, go back and start there. Enjoy!

Editing: Rose Santoriello

Proofreading: Lauren, Madeline & Emily

Cover Art: Amanda Hawkins, Eternal Geekery

This book is for 18+

 Created with Vellum

To those who have stayed with shitty men
longer than they should have
and then found the courage to leave...
This is for you and me.
They were never worthy of us anyway.

Before you read...

This book contains adult themes such as explicit sex scenes, a breakup, misogyny, mild homophobia, brief mention of a spouse who has died (neither of the main characters), mention of parents who have died (one of the main characters' parents died when they were a child), and more. This book is intended for mature audiences, and reader discretion is advised. If you have any concerns about the content of this book, feel free to email the author, Madison Nicole, at info@ madisonnicolebooks.com. Your mental health matters.

ONE

Jake screamed at the TV, something about a random person being an asshole for killing him in his game. His dark hair was messy, and his sweats hung low on his hips, exposing the tanned skin of his muscled abdominals and chest. Once upon a time, he had been a dream—the epitome of what a woman should want. Of what I'd thought I wanted.

A knight in shining armor, except I had never needed one. My independence was always more important. I was the one who had a house, a thriving career, and a beautiful group of friends. It seemed all that was missing was a handsome suitor at my feet. The picture of a perfect life, I just needed a love interest to complete my happily ever after. There was a time when I'd thought he was the missing piece.

Even thinking those things made me cringe. I felt stupid and naive for falling into the trap of thinking I needed a partner to make my life fulfilling. Now, it felt like Jake was all that was wrong in my life. Maybe that wasn't fair, but it held a decent amount of truth. He wasn't what I wanted anymore. The emotional and mental labor needed to keep him alive felt like I signed up for a child instead of a partner. The urge to strangle him was way more present than the desire to be intimate with him. My daydreams were about being alone now, without the weight of an absent, pretty-boy boyfriend.

I watched him, engrossed in his game, and felt nothing but annoyance and irritation. There was a time when I loved him. We had years together where I'd thought he was the one, but then I realized I was queer. He had taken it in stride, acting like it wasn't a big deal even though I was grappling between the identities of bi, pan, and queer. It didn't really matter to him because we would be together forever, he'd said. As if that didn't fundamentally exist in my DNA—as if the suppression of it for years was no big deal. It was difficult to explain how momentous it was and how I was a changed person because of it. But he didn't really understand.

That was the start and end of that conversation with him. Otherwise, he liked to pretend I was who I always was: a straight, half-Korean, half-Russian girl, who was only interested in a hunky, straight, white, handsome bro-dude. That the evolution of my identity didn't matter to our everyday lives.

How do you explain that to someone who has no idea what it means to be confused by the things they think and feel?

My whole friend group was queer, and it was celebrated and normalized in a way I seemed to be missing in my intimate relationship. I couldn't put my finger on exactly what was missing, but I knew for certain this wasn't actually supporting my individuality.

It made me think of my parents and their own love story. My heart ached in the best way. I remembered asking them a million times when I was a small child about how they'd met. It was like a fairy-tale story coming to life—a beautiful circus love story that was basically meant to be a movie.

They both worked on a show overseas together. Two

acrobats who fell in love from two different places. A match made in heaven. Now they were retired and came to shows when they could, but mostly they traveled the world, still obsessed with each other and lending support when I asked for it. Neither one of their families were excited about the circus, despite both Russia and Korea having deep roots in performance arts. It had always just been the three of us growing up in the States. They had settled down here after their amazing career. My parents had gone out with a bang, making their last shows a dedication and homage to their story. I cried every time I watched their final performance, and then still shed a few tears when I would replay some of their acts in my head.

They were, of course, not surprised at all I was queer. The circus fostered deep-rooted inclusion for everyone, and that's what they'd grown up in. They loved me no matter what and just wanted me to be happy. After I was eventually set up with Cirque Callisto and had bought my house, they took off on their own adventure, wishing me well and chatting when they could. Even from miles away, I could feel their support, which was why it didn't make a damn bit of sense that Jake was feet away from me, yet I didn't feel shit from him.

My heart yearned for a love like theirs. Was that really too much to ask for?

The last few months, Jake's effort in our relationship had taken a magnificent cliff dive and somehow was now buried six feet underground. He stopped showing up for me in the ways I needed him most. The house was mine, but he lived here too, and I was sick and tired of being treated like someone's maid, chef, and unlimited money supply. He had no inclination to help with anything, and I didn't know why I tolerated it. Sometimes it felt like my fault, like I had allowed it to happen, but he had made those choices. My mind was a mess, vacillating from blaming myself to putting it all on him.

I felt like his freaking caretaker, and it made me want to light something on fire.

"Hey." I interrupted my thoughts as I stood in the doorway. He didn't hear me, so I walked closer to the TV, but he barely spared me a second glance. Was I just invisible? So easy to cast aside when all I wanted was to have a genuine conversation? It felt like I didn't matter, and that was like a punch to my stomach.

"Jake," I said, projecting confidence into my voice even though my insides felt like Jell-O. The urge to scream or cry hit my body like a tidal wave and threatened to knock me over. I needed to have this conversation without emotionally melting in front of him.

I can do this. Deep breaths. In and out.

"Myla, I'm in the middle of a game!" he whined before cheering about something that happened with his buddies in his headphones.

"Yes, I can see that it's very important," I drawled sarcastically, but it barely registered for him. My belly started to heat with rage, and I ground my teeth together. I could fucking do this. I didn't want to be a coward. Today, I would not let him walk all over me.

"We can talk later?" He grinned at the screen, and it made me want nothing more than to rip the cord from the outlet and stomp on his headphones, wiping that smug smirk off his face.

"No, we can't. I have a performance tonight. You know, with the show I've been doing for the past month you *still* haven't bothered to see." He became uninterested in my shows a while ago. Even though my parents weren't here, they watched every recording they could get their hands on. He couldn't even do that, let alone show up in person. I couldn't remember the last time he had championed my art. This was my life, for god's sake. I liked to think I was an interesting person. Circus was fun and exciting! Most people would be delighted to support their partner's creativity, but not mine. Mine would rather sit on his ass and basically ignore me until he wanted something from me.

Other people would ask, "Where's Jake?" and I would come up with the dumbest excuses. Eventually, people stopped bringing it up, except my nosy and loving besties. The shame that would heat my cheeks every time I stumbled through an answer was usually met with empathetic eyes and a caring hug. I always knew they wanted to press me more, but they never did. Sometimes I wish they would, and other times I wanted to run away crying. They were waiting for me to admit it to myself out loud, but the words always got caught in my throat.

"Hold on, guys. Give me a minute." He paused whatever he was doing and looked at me, both corners of his mouth curving up.

My face was blank. "Are you ever going to come to this show?"

"Come on, My, I've been to plenty of your shows." He sat back and huffed out a breath, looking like a petulant child. Food wrappers and takeout containers were littered around him, and I wondered why he decided to stop trying in this relationship. Was it a conscious choice, or one he made passively? Either way, it wasn't fair to me.

"And I will continue to do new shows, and I want to share that with the person I'm dating. If I were a football player, your butt would be at every game," I said, trying to keep my voice even and calm despite the storm brewing in my body.

Scowling, he shrugged. "That would be different. I love football."

I refrained from shouting in his face. "And you don't love supporting me? Do you not love me?"

"Myla, not this again," he groaned, like this argument was

silly and not absolutely life-altering. You did things for the people you loved, even if they weren't your favorite, right? That was the normal thing to do. Did he think I liked picking up after him or picking up his slack around the house? No. But I did it because we were supposed to be a team.

"Fine. Don't come. You know what you can do instead? Clean the house and pay me back all the money I lent you," I bit out. I didn't have time for this fight. I needed to get going. I needed to get ready for tonight. But my emotions threatened to burst out of me anytime I looked at him lately. I wanted this fight with him, but I sure as heck didn't have time for it now.

"You know I'm short on money right now. I'm not getting put on as many shifts. Business has been slow."

I was the artist. If anyone was short on money, it should have been me. But, instead, I was the responsible adult who actually saved, budgeted, and worked my butt off to have my shit together. There was a time in my life when I was working at eight different places; the least he could do was cover his half and get another part-time job.

And where the hell was his money going? He never left the house, and he barely offered to cover anything between the two of us. What happened to the savings he used to boast about?

"It's been slow for several months, Jake. I already pay for all the utilities and the food you eat. If you can't pay your half, then you need to find another job." Was I shrieking right now? It felt like I was slowly unraveling at the seams, and Jake was content with watching me fall apart.

"Babe, I'm working on it," he groused, his bright-blue eyes pleading and his bottom lip sticking out in a pout.

"Are you, though? Because it feels like you just do this all day, every day." I waved at his game. He had no boundaries with it, and it absolutely consumed his life. I was all for escapism, but Jake desperately needed a reality check. Lots of people could play video games and have a job. Why exactly was that difficult for him?

"Just give me another month or two, and I promise things will be good." He went to grab his headphones and put them back on. Suddenly a mental image of me shoving them in the garbage disposal consumed me, and it brought me just the smallest kernel of joy.

"I guess we're just done with this conversation?" I wanted to throw something at him. My whole body hurt from how aggressively I was clenching.

"Don't you need to go to your show?" He nodded at the bag I was death-gripping in my hands. He was right. This couldn't happen right now. I took my job seriously, and I really hated being late, especially for something like this.

"I do. I'll see you later, then." Stomping out, I slammed the door to the sound of him getting back on to greet his buddies. Throwing my bag in my car, I shot off a quick text to Logan saying I was on my way and apologizing for being late. She would understand. Logan always did.

Angry tears fell down my face, and I swiped at them with my hands. Thank god I hadn't done my makeup yet, or it would have been ruined. I couldn't keep doing this with him. I felt so alone, even with him there.

It wasn't that bad being my partner, was it? Lots of people thought I was fun and interesting. People loved coming to my shows, and other people had partners who were devoted to seeing them every weekend. The urge to call my parents and be comforted by them was strong, but I didn't want to bother them while they were in... I didn't even know where they were. France? Maybe Germany? My head felt cloudy, fogging my memory.

My phone dinged and, as if I had summoned them, there was a good-luck message from my parents with a selfie of them kissing in front of the Louvre, and the tears fell down my face even harder.

I wasn't even asking for much. I just wanted him to come see *one* show. Being a performer was a hard-ass job, and I had worked relentlessly to do this full time. Why couldn't he just do the bare minimum for our life together?

I drove, trying to let muscle memory take over and calm the raging tsunami in my body. I wasn't doing a very good job of it, though. Being this keyed up for my performance wasn't good. My body needed to be centered and calm in order to go on stage, not one second from collapsing and sobbing.

Checking my face in the mirror, I tried to take a few deep breaths before I left my car and walked into the dressing room. My friends would see right through me, but I could pretend it wasn't a big deal as long as it didn't look like I had just been bawling my eyes out. This is what I did—I put on a show, even if it was my life.

Exhaling, I told myself to get it together, because we had a performance to do. This was my job, and I needed to do it. I pushed open the doors to the theater and made my way into our dressing room where Logan, Aven, and Jess were already standing.

As soon as I walked in, they all whipped around to look at me. I gave my best dazzling smile. It was an absolute, catastrophic fail of a happy, smiling face. I winced, cracking the mask I was desperately clinging to.

"Myla…" Logan started, and my smile slid off my lips. Then I burst into tears all over again, and they all rushed around me.

"Shhh, it's okay. We're here for you," Jess cooed, her warm, familiar vanilla scent comforting me.

"Cry it out, babe." Aven stroked my hair gently.

"Men are so stupid!" I cried out to no one in particular.

"They really are," Logan soothed and handed me some tissues as I blew my nose aggressively.

"Jake and I aren't doing too good. I want to destroy his Xbox," I confessed, and they giggled.

"I take it he won't be coming to the show?" Jess asked, handing me some water. I nodded.

"He said he's seen too many of my shows. Why does he have to see this one?" My body shook as I cried even harder.

"Because you're a hottie who is incredibly talented and deserves to be seen again and again and again." Aven held my face in her hands and stared into my soul. I searched her hazel eyes like they could give me the answer to this Jake problem, but all I saw was what I already knew. This *needed* to end, yet I wasn't sure I was ready. I wasn't strong enough to kick him out. Instead, I continued to snuffle.

"Yeah but he doesn't want to support me," I said, gulping down air. I tried to get myself together and was doing a terrible job of not leaking more tears.

"Myla, are there other things going on?" Logan asked, her arms crossed and fire lit her eyes.

"Yeah." What was I supposed to say? That the guy I'd fallen in love with wasn't really there anymore? That I was sick and tired of letting him walk all over me when he gave absolutely nothing in return? My friends were all badasses and said whatever they wanted with confidence. Yet here I was hiding from my emotions and the hard truth that I needed to leave this relationship but somehow couldn't.

"He doesn't deserve you," Logan said quietly, like the words might scare me.

"I don't know what to do," I whispered.

"You don't have to do anything right now. Let's get you cleaned up and ready to go so you can go out on that stage and do what you love. We'll help you figure out Jake after, okay? You're a strong, independent woman who doesn't need a man!" Jess said with conviction. Easy for her to say considering she was a hot lesbian who had women fawning all over her, including her ex.

"I know. I need to do something about him, but I just don't know what. We've been together for years. How do you extract yourself from that?" This was too much right now. I couldn't think about ending things at this exact moment in time, could I?

"You just need to make it through the next few hours. You can do this, Myla. Then we will devour a whole tub of cookie dough and make a plan for how to get you out of this." Aven began styling my hair as Logan sat me down and started on my makeup. I just nodded and let them fuss. They would take care of me no matter what, even if that meant I stayed with a shitty guy like Jake.

The show went off without a hitch, and I got tons of cheers for my aerial silks solo. The people loved the big drops and spins and splits. I moved through the performance like I was floating. My body went on autopilot, and I did what I needed to do.

Afterward, my friends tried to get me to come over and talk it out, but my body and heart were spent, so I drove home in silence. I needed time to think and breathe. When I got back to my house, Jake had fallen asleep on the couch. Normally, I would wake him up and tell him to come to bed, but not tonight. I didn't want him anywhere near me.

I curled up in my bed and thought about how I was going to get through tomorrow, when all I needed was to be left alone.

Two

"That was marvelous, Dani!" A woman beamed up at me, and I grinned back politely.

"Thank you," I said, wanting to go anywhere but here and sit in silence with the lights off, but unfortunately I *needed* to network. It was part of my job to be available after shows. Even if what I really wanted was to decompress and put on soft, flowy pants.

"What a fantastic last performance!" another patron said. I nodded, trying to slip away into the crowd. Slowly, the other performers joined me as we looked at our generous donor, Mrs. Williams. It wasn't her fault I was overstimulated. I tried my best to lock down my discomfort and put on a mask.

"You all did marvelous, and I'm incredibly thankful for all your hard work." She dabbed at her eyes with a worn handkerchief. This woman had to be at least seventy years old, and she poured all her old money into the arts community. I was grateful for her investment in us, but that didn't fix my social anxiety. I looked to see what everyone else was doing and tried my best to replicate their elated faces.

"It has been wonderful to work with and for you, ma'am."

Our director, Katie, bowed her head, and we all clapped as Mrs. Williams blushed.

She went through and thanked every individual performer. She was truly a gem, and we were lucky to have someone who loved and cherished us as people, not just performers. Not everyone had donors like that, and it was nice of her to stop by after the show and congratulate us personally.

"Dani, do you have a second?" Katie waved me over, away from the rest of the company.

"What's up?" My social cup was already depleted. I desperately hoped this conversation would be short and to the point.

"I wanted to check in and see how you are doing. And see what your plans are after this. I know you only signed a contract for this show, but we would love for you to stay and be a part of our regular performance schedule, if you want." Katie looked at me with wide, hopeful eyes.

"That's an incredible offer. I don't have plans right now, but I've really enjoyed my time with you and the company. This show has been incredibly rewarding. Do you mind if I think about it?" I tugged on my ear mindlessly, wanting to take off this costume and this makeup immediately.

"Of course, no pressure. I'll send you an email with all the details of what we can offer you and a timeline that works for us. We've really enjoyed your talent and character, Dani. We would be honored to have you!" She gave me a quick, hard squeeze, then went off to greet the rest of the audience.

The truth was, this company was great. Katie was kind, and the performers were professional and hardworking. But it didn't feel like where I was supposed to be exactly. I had a restlessness in me that didn't seem satisfied to stay here. My plan had never been to settle in this place, but to be here for as long as I was needed and then go on my way.

I lingered for as little as was appropriate, trying to stay on the outskirts of the crowd. But a few people snagged me to take a few photos with some of the audience members of our show. We were lucky to have such a dedicated community around us who loved the arts and contributed to our sold-out shows. God, I wished I was better at this part, but small talk made me want to squirm, and I was close to running away from the noise in here. Truthfully, in the short term, I needed to get out of here and get comfortable. Long term, I felt like I needed something else entirely.

I was ready for a new adventure. Maybe I would go back to Spain, where my grandparents lived, and look for something there. The idea flooded my body with warmth, but I wasn't sure if that was the answer. Or maybe I would go somewhere where I had no ties, like Thailand or Brazil.

An upsetting thought pierced my brain. Was I running away or toward something? It was hard for me to say. There wasn't any urgency from anyone but me. It was my own monster chasing me to something new.

This show had given me grace to explore and create, really perfecting my flute and straps acts, as well as some of my clowning. A new challenge sounded fun and exciting. This could be exactly what I needed. I just didn't know if now was the time or what exactly those next steps looked like. I needed to see what Katie would offer, then broaden my horizons to see what else was available.

Kind words were exchanged between the other performers, and a lot of them were going out to celebrate the final run. It wasn't my thing, though, therefore I politely declined. Instead, I took the drive back to my brother's house slowly, trying to think of what to do next. Lately, it seemed like every day I was being existential. Sometimes, I had to remind myself I had nothing but time. The sense of immediacy that shoved at my back didn't need to be there. It was often just society's expectations and my personal rigidity that kept my mind racing. Both of which were difficult for me to shake off.

"I'm home!" I hollered as I walked in, and Macy, my brother's adorable little wiener dog, greeted me. "Hi, Macy. Where's everyone else?" I cooed at her and gave her some belly rubs. She looked up at me adoringly with dark-brown eyes, and a little bit of the tension in my shoulders released.

"We're in the living room!" my brother yelled. I snatched a snack from the fridge and made my way toward them, where my brother was sitting on the floor in front of the couch while my niece put butterfly clips in his hair.

"Daddy is my beauty queen tonight," Lily said proudly as she clipped and unclipped chunks of my brother's dirty-blonde hair. He looked absolutely wild.

"And he is very pretty." I tried to stifle my giggle at how ridiculous my brother looked with makeup smeared all across his face like a watercolor painting. Lily had really done a number on him, and I had to admire her craft.

"Dani, you already look pretty," Lily said, pausing and looking at me. Her hair was in two dark pigtail braids that looked just like her mom's, and she had blue eyes that looked just like my brother's.

"Thank you. It was the last day of my show, so I had to dress up." I did a little twirl as she oohed and ahhed at me. I hadn't bothered to take off my makeup or mess with my hair after the show. Instead, I had put on different clothes and sprinted out of there to listen to my music in my car with no one else around me.

"Daddy said we couldn't go for some reason." She pouted, abandoning the clips and patting the couch for me to sit on.

"I know. It was sort of an adult-only thing. But one of these days, you'll get to come and see me at other shows." I gave her a little squeeze, and she giggled. My brother had made it to the show opening weekend, but it was definitely not child friendly. It was already bad enough my brother was there while I was wearing nipple tassels and other performers were throwing dildos around. Most of my shows were not like this, but even if they were, Soaren would be supportive.

"Do you fly like you do in your videos?" she asked, bright-eyed. Lily loved seeing my training videos and said one day she would learn how to soar, too.

"Yeah, just like my videos." I tickled her side, and she laughed wildly.

"Okay, Lily, it's way past your bedtime. I said we could wait for Dani, and we did." My brother's tone was stern, but I knew he would cave if she whined enough. He had a hard time saying no to her, and I really couldn't blame him.

"Okay, Daddy." She gave me one last squeeze as they headed to bed.

"I love you, Lily. Sweet dreams!" I called out as my brother carried her out.

"I love you, Dani!" she proclaimed.

While they went through her bedtime routine, I grabbed some more food and caught up on Instagram and my emails. The show had run for several months, and it was truly the end of a beautiful performance. The final show was always a little bittersweet; a sense of melancholy that stuck to my skin and made my eyes prickle.

Maybe I would stay. My brother could always use the help, and I loved being here even though it wasn't exactly what I wanted. The communities here were just not exactly my people. I was still looking for that place that felt just right. They were all nice enough, but I felt like the odd one out most of the time despite their kindness.

Scrolling on Instagram, I saw Cirque Callisto calling for guest artists. I had worked with Logan before. She was a badass, so that could be interesting. I knew they were very queer, and that made my heart do a little happy dance.

Logan was known for not taking any shit and welcoming everyone from all walks of life with open arms. There were whispers, especially among the male circus artists, that she would chew you up and spit you out if you threatened, harassed, or harmed any of her performers. She wasn't someone you wanted to cross. However, if you were part of her family, Logan would go to the ends of the earth to protect you. It sounded like somewhere that I could really settle in, too.

My current company was wonderful, but there weren't a ton of queer people here, which was a bit tough. Everyone was respectful of my pronouns and my identities, but it wasn't that same sense of community queer spaces provided for other queer folks.

"How was the last show?" My brother came in, wiping his face with a baby wipe.

"God, Lily did a number on you." I laughed fully now that she had gone to bed. He was a great sport about it. I was proud of the dad he was; Lily was in great hands with him.

"Tell me about it." The corners of his mouth tipped up as he continued to rub off the red lipstick.

"It was good. They asked if I wanted to stay longer for the next show. Not sure for how long, but they pay well and seemed enthusiastic about me doing another round of shows with them." My voice fell a little flat. Job security was obviously ideal, but I couldn't get myself to be excited about it. The money was tempting, but I knew in my soul this wasn't the opportunity for me. I knew my enthusiasm sounded forced and fake. Soaren could sniff it from a mile away. He knew me better than anyone else, sometimes even better than I knew myself.

"And what did you say?" He sat down across from where I was eating at the kitchen table.

"I asked for time to think about it." I picked at my food in front of me.

"Do you want to stay, Dani?" Soaren asked gently. Even though he probably already knew the answer.

"I don't know. I have a lot of confusing emotions about it. I've loved being here with you and Lily, but I don't think this is it for me." I pulled at my ear and looked into Soaren's understanding eyes.

"I know. I never expected you to be here long. I appreciated you coming when I called all those months ago. Since Millie's passing, it's been tough being a single dad. You've always been my best friend, Dani, but we can manage on our own now. You helped a lot this past year, and I know it's been a lot. We would love it if you stayed, and we will love you if you go. You will always have a home here, and if you leave, it will give us an excuse to go visit someplace else." Soaren's eyes were watery as he spoke.

Tears welled in my eyes. "Are you sure you and Lily will be okay?"

"Yes. We're in a much better place now. Therapy, medication, and a whole slew of other things have helped me find myself again to be a better dad and brother. Our foundations are strong, and we can survive without you being here." He nodded, swiping at his eyes.

God, he was such a good dad and brother. I was really proud of how far he had come this past year. Grief was a bitch, and I couldn't imagine what it was like to lose the love of your life. It was already tough losing our parents at such a young age. Our grandparents in the States had rushed over to where we'd lived to raise us in our childhood home, and then in the summers we'd go visit our other grandparents in Spain. It was a wonderful childhood in many ways but incredibly hard in others.

Now, it was just the two of us here with Lily. Life was an

absolute bitch sometimes, and it seemed to hand out grief in large handfuls to Soaren and me. We had both done a lot of work to be able to live with what that meant. Every day was a little different.

There was a part of me that felt like if I left, I would be abandoning him. But he had made roots here with friends and his own career and community. I knew he would be okay. I just wanted to really make sure he could handle it before I uprooted myself for my selfish desires.

"I love you both very much, but I think I just need a new start somewhere. But if you need anything, you can always call, and I'll come running back, okay? You're my family, and I wouldn't abandon you." I walked over and gave him a big hug.

"Where do you think you will go?" he asked, holding me tight.

"I'm not sure yet. There's another circus company I've been interested in for a while I want to check out. They just posted a listing for guest artists for a new show, and I know the creative director—we trained together before. I'm wondering if they're looking for any more full-time or part-time residents." I could always see how it went, then try out somewhere else if I didn't like it.

That was the beauty of this work—I could move and be free without the confines of a regular nine-to-five. Plus, I had a decent amount of money saved up from living with my brother for free and babysitting Lily, as well as consuming all their food.

"I think you should try it out. You can always ask for financial help, too. Your big brother is more than happy to share." Soaren grinned at me, and I rolled my eyes.

"Yes, the capitalist hellscape of this earth does tend to pay corporate lawyers very well," I teased. He was incredibly generous with his money and privilege since we were our own little family unit. Anything I needed, he had provided since I'd moved in with them to help with Lily after Millie's passing.

She had been a wonderful woman full of life and love. I had loved her like my sister. The world was a cruel place to take someone like that away.

"It's the least I can do. But, Dani, wherever you go, we will stand by you. You have saved me numerous times over. I'm happy to return the favor again and again."

Tears slipped down my cheeks at his confession.

"Okay, I'll reach out to this other company and see what they say."

"They would be lucky to have you."

I hoped he was right. Otherwise, I didn't know where else I would end up. I was confident whatever happened would be meant to be.

THREE

"Myla, what do you want for dinner?" Jake leaned against the kitchen counter while scrolling through his phone.

"Maybe Thai or something?" What I really wanted was for dinner to be ready when I got home after having a long day. My body was aching, and I just wanted to sink into a bath and drink a glass of wine. But I needed nourishment to keep myself going. Consequently, I supposed food was necessary. Jake never had the foresight to do anything nice for me. If I didn't make dinner or tell him exactly what I wanted, nothing would be there for me when I got home.

I had brought up before, several times, that it would be nice if he could do a bit more around the house. He always said, "Yeah, of course." It would change for a few days, then go right back to how it used to be. I didn't want to nag, but it was hurtful. Maybe I just needed to accept it. This was just one of those things I didn't love about him, but everyone had stuff like that in relationships, right?

Sometimes I desperately wanted the mental load to be less. The emotional labor of constantly making every decision and holding the reins in this relationship was exhausting, especially when Jake wasn't even working. Conflicting emotions flitted through my head. I should be kind and empathetic to his situation. Relationships weren't always fifty-fifty; right now, I was just doing more so he could figure himself out.

Part of me felt guilty for wanting the mess that was our situation to go away. If this was how our relationship was going to be for the rest of our lives, I didn't think I could do it. This wasn't fulfilling, and I wasn't sure how long I should keep trying to fix this, because maybe it would always be broken.

"Eh, I don't really want that." Jake scrunched up his face.

His reaction was like a match that lit a fire in my belly I couldn't extinguish. Resentment curled its way through my body. This was small. By all means, this should not matter. Deciding on dinner plans was not that big of a deal. However, the past few months seemed to be a constant stream of discussions I would start and then eventually let go of because they got me nowhere. Trying to have a conversation with him about our relationship was like talking to a brick wall.

Why was I doing this? What was I actually getting out of this relationship? Clearing my throat, I tried to focus on the task at hand: food.

"What do you want, then?" I asked. My goal was to make it come out kind and soft, but it was edgy and broken. He seemed unfazed, which irritated me even more.

"Maybe pizza or something?" he offered.

His favorite. Not mine. Why was that bothersome to me? This was just food.

"Fine," I grumbled, just wanting to get into my bath and stuff something in my face. This was how it always went, though. I would concede to keep peace between us and not bring up what I actually wanted and needed. My feelings would be shoved down again because no matter what I said or did, nothing ever changed. When did I become overly passive? Was I always like this?

My mind tried to pick out the exact moment in time I stopped asking for what I needed in this relationship. Who could I really blame but myself? He wasn't a mind reader. Maybe when I brought things up, I was too nice. This was a problem I could solve. I could be more assertive.

"Cool. Can I have your card?" He looked at me expectantly, and the budding irritation in my belly grew hot. We had talked about this. He was supposed to pay for more things because I was already paying for more than half our stuff. We'd literally *just* talked about this. Why was he backsliding immediately?

"Why don't you use yours?" I placed my hands on my hips and tried to quell the angry tears threatening to spill down my cheeks. Angry crying was the worst. People thought tears always mean sadness, but in reality, I was so pissed my body could only express it through tears.

My watery eyes then landed on a box shoved next to the TV, like someone had tried to hide it in a half-assed way. It was for the latest PlayStation console, with a pile of accessories next to it. He couldn't pay for our dinner tonight, but he could pay for a whole new gaming setup?

Are you kidding me?

"You know I don't have a lot of cash right now." He shrugged his shoulders like it wasn't a big deal. And I had to fight back the urge to scream *liar* right in his face. This wasn't me. When had this anger grown so exponentially I was ready to explode?

"But I thought you got another job?" My throat hurt from how much I was holding back an angry sob. I knew he wasn't working a lot, but I didn't realize it had filtered down to not working at all. God, how did I end up in this mess with him? How had I allowed it to get this bad? Was this all my fault? A poor excuse of a partner who couldn't say what was in her heart?

No, this wasn't all me.

Jake had played an active part in this, and it wasn't my responsibility to hold his hand through adult life. No one had held mine. This wasn't something I had to put up with anymore if I didn't want to.

"It didn't pan out." He didn't look too broken up about it.

"Why haven't you gotten another one? And why didn't you tell me?"

"Uh, because the job market is hard out there, and I didn't think it was that big a deal," he said. His cavalier attitude only made mine worse.

"But we talked about this..." I whispered, and he rolled his eyes at me.

"Come on, Myla. Why are you being such a bitch about this? Just pay for dinner!" Jake yelled, and I gasped, taking a step back.

"What did you just call me?" It was like a punch to the gut.

"I don't know why, but you're being a bitch." Jake crossed his arms in front of his chest, and the anger simmering in my blood moments ago went to a full-on boil. I clutched the countertop and swayed slightly.

My friends had said it, and I needed to finally listen. There was no way I could do this anymore. I was done. Five seconds of courage, and I could get out the words I had desperately needed to say for way too long.

That was the last straw. I didn't care what his situation was anymore. Our priorities were not the same. This sham of a relationship needed to end. Now.

"Jake." I clenched my fists so hard I was sure my fingernails would leave marks. He was still scowling at me like his words were just and right. As if calling your girlfriend a bitch was a totally normal thing to do.

"What?" He looked dumbfounded and a little irritated that pizza was not on its way to us.

It was like a switch had flipped inside me. "I don't want this anymore," I blurted. A spark of relief brushed over me, and I was hooked. Was it possible to actually feel this way? I latched onto that sensation and held on for my life, hoping it wouldn't get lost in my anger and hurt.

"I mean, fine, we don't have to get pizza, but I don't want Thai," he grumbled, then went back to scrolling on his phone.

"Not the food. I don't want this. Us." Oh no, I really didn't want to cry right now. In my heart, I cupped that little flame of hope and relief and tried to protect it with my whole being.

Say what you need to say, Myla. Don't lose your nerve now.

"You're breaking up with me over this stupid little fight?" he asked, like it wasn't a big deal. Like that's all that it was. As if our relationship hadn't died months ago. The grave had been dug, and I had refused to acknowledge it. He had taken a back seat to the life we had together and, for far too long, I dragged him along like dead weight trying to keep us together. "Or is it about the money?"

"No, Jake. It's the lack of commitment. The lack of enthusiasm to be with me. You calling me a bitch and not giving a damn. And yes, it's about the money. But it's more than that. It's about my queer identity. The inability to get your shit together. The fact you have no motivation to make any fucking changes," I yelled at him, wanting to release the pressure that had been building around my heart. Something needed to give in, and it had to be him. I would no longer allow it to be me. "And frankly, I don't love you anymore. Not after all this."

"You're abandoning me in my time of need?" His eyes flashed with hurt, then anger.

Was he actually serious right now?

"You have been mooching off me for months. I tried to help you, but you can't even help yourself, Jake." I flung my hands out, and a small weight on my chest slid away. Finally, I could breathe again. My little flame of hope grew. I could do this. It was now or never. This time, I would say what I wanted and mean it. I would be free.

Keep going, Myla. Don't stop now.

"This isn't fair, Myla. You know I'm a good guy. I've just been in a rough patch." He pouted like a petulant child, and I wanted to throw something at him. That had worked in the past, but not tonight. Not anymore.

"And we all struggle. But it isn't my job to fix this for you. We all have our own stuff. I have never expected you to solve things for me while I did nothing to figure it out." I stalked toward him and got right up in his face. Let's see how much of a bitch I could actually be.

"You're angry. Let's just sleep on this, and then we can talk about it tomorrow." He searched my eyes like an answer might be there, as if I would crawl back into a docile hole and concede like I had been doing for months.

Not gonna happen, buddy. This ends today.

"No." It felt good coming out of my mouth. Powerful. I would no longer sit by and watch him stomp on my desires.

"Please, Myla, you're not thinking straight. You had a bad day, and you're taking it out on me."

"Don't tell me how to feel, Jake," I hissed at him, grabbing a bottle of wine and popping the cork.

"It's okay. This is just a little fight, and we will get over it. I'll do more, I promise. I'll get a couple part-time jobs and do the dishes more and play video games less. I'll go out looking first thing tomorrow. I'm sorry I called you a bitch, baby." He beamed like this was the solution. As if his apology was perfect.

He had the features of the all-American boy—tall, tanned, and handsome. A smile that could promise you things that would never come true. The words out of his mouth didn't hold an ounce of truth. He couldn't deliver on anything, and it was time I finally accepted that.

"Is this what you want? Do you even love me anymore? We haven't slept together in months, and you've been sleeping on the couch for quite some time." Maybe I could reason with him to see this was going south for both of us. Maybe it would help him get the heck out of my house.

"I just fall asleep out here after playing my games. I didn't realize it was such a big deal," he said, looking like I was making a mountain out of a molehill. But that was the thing —relationships were about little things. Your partner should care about the small stuff. Because otherwise they turned into big, ugly problems.

"It's not just that. It's the fact I'm fine with it. I would rather not have you near me. The thought of us having sex again seems implausible and repulsive." The fire inside me consumed me like an inferno. The words I had held back for months were spilling out; even if they were hurtful, they had to be said.

"You don't mean that." His bottom lip wobbled, and I refrained from laughing in his face. This sad-little-puppy-dog act had run its course. He had literally just insulted me moments ago, and he thought this would work?

"Do you love me anymore?" I asked again, wanting to know the answer even though it didn't really matter. I poured myself a glass of wine to try and get my hands to stop trembling from all the emotions flowing out of me.

"Of course I still love you." He stepped toward me, but I ducked away.

"I don't believe you."

"What is that supposed to mean? You won't even let me touch you." He slammed his phone down and threw an accusatory finger at me.

"Yes, because when someone loves someone else, they work together to find a solution because they're partners. They support one another. Their dreams, their careers, everything. But you haven't done any of that for a long time." God, this wine tasted almost as good as the words spewing from my lips.

"Sorry I haven't been obsessed with you. I have my life too," he groused.

"No, you really don't." Sighing, I tried to think of the best way to get him out of here. I needed a plan, and fast.

"I take my apology back. You are being a real bitch today," Jake spat at me.

My whole body flinched on impact from that word again. You know what? He had no idea what I was capable of and, even though I had lost my way for a while, you bet your ass I was back on track now. No more of this. I would not be a side character to my freaking life.

"Here's what's going to happen—I'm going to order my own food for dinner without you." I was gathering courage, anger, and my fire of hope to finish this once and for all.

He scoffed and rolled his eyes.

"Then I'm going to go to my room because this is *my house* and take a bubble bath with this bottle of wine."

His eyes narrowed at me, and he pursed his lips.

"And you will be sleeping on the couch tonight because by the time I get up tomorrow, you will need to be gone. You are no longer welcome here. We are over. You are done living here and you need to go be someone else's problem."

TAKE. THAT. Mentally, I did a little victory dance that involved shaking my butt and pumping my fists in the air.

"How the fuck am I supposed to be gone by tomorrow morning?"

"I don't know, and I really don't care." Grabbing my phone, I ordered delivery from my favorite place. It said it would be here in forty-five minutes.

"You'll change your mind tomorrow, Myla. I'm not leaving." He sat down on the couch and huffed in frustration.

"If I wake up tomorrow and you are not actively moving your junk out of here, there will be hell to pay. Do you understand?" My body began trembling again, and the angry tears pricked the backs of my eyes. I had made it this far and I would be damned if I shed those tears now.

"What are you going to do about it, Myla? I have a right to be here, because this is my home too, you know."

My mouth dropped open. "You really don't. First off, because I own this house, and second, you are not simply entitled to things because I have allowed you to be here."

"You can't kick me out." He ignored everything I said.

"Watch me." I stomped away and avoided him the rest of the evening. He made no moves to pack his things. He simply got back to playing his video games and yelling at the TV.

Now that my emotions had settled and my adrenaline had cooled, I felt exhausted. How was I going to get him out of here? I nibbled on my nails as I slipped into my bath.

I would need my people. They could help me. If tomorrow morning he was still here, I would call in the calvary.

The warmth of the bath settled me enough in my conviction that no matter what, Jake would need to be gone tomorrow. I was done with him and his bullshit.

If he couldn't show up for me and respect me, then he would need to show himself out. With that thought, I let the bubbles and wine comfort me, hoping tomorrow he would make my life easy and just be gone.

FOUR

My bones felt heavy in my body, but in the good kind of way. I had missed laughing hard, my stomach aching, and playing intensely in a studio setting. It was amazing how easy it was to fall in with the company here. Logan was a fantastic leader and artist. Everyone here seemed to be a whole bunch of queer weirdos who just wanted to live their lives and do odd shit.

I still needed to figure out my living situation. It wasn't ideal to be staying with one of my brother's friends from college. He and his girlfriend were fine, but I felt like I was infringing on their space and it made me feel... not great. But it was the easiest and most convenient option at the moment. I hadn't wanted to ask too much of Logan before I even got here even though she had offered her own place for me to stay for just a few weeks. She had already been incredibly generous and kind, and I didn't want to take advantage of that.

It was hard sometimes—accepting people wanted me in their space and I wouldn't be a burden on them. Instead I told her it was fine; I had a temporary situation and I just needed some time to figure out what I wanted to do.

Living by myself wasn't a bad idea, but all the studio apartments around here were expensive, and I barely had any furniture. Something about living alone, too, wasn't calling to me. I wanted at least one other human around, but being new in the city meant friends and roommates were hard to come by. My natural inclination wasn't to be the loudest or most bubbly in a room, so trying to snatch a long-term roommate up would be tough business.

However, I was on Facebook roommate groups almost every day looking for a good situation. Nothing had really caught my eye thus far, so the search would continue. Maybe I could ask Logan if she knew of anyone in the company or any of their friends who might need a roommate? Ideally it would be something that could work out for a while, not just a couple months. A recommendation from her seemed like a way better option than trying to sift through random people in a Facebook group.

On the bright side, I was able to have creative freedom with my acts and my music. But due to my living situation, I wasn't sure what the rules were about me playing my instruments. Of course Mark and Ashley had acted like it wasn't a big deal, but I felt incredibly loud and intrusive whenever I did. That could have been my own head trash, but I certainly didn't feel like the noise was welcome. There was no way I would be able to teach students here either, because students at the beginning of their musical journey were agonizing to listen to. Especially if you weren't used to it.

Lying down on my bed, my brother FaceTimed me, and I was more than happy to answer.

"Hi, Soaren!" I said excitedly as Lily shoved her face into the camera. "Hi, Lily, you've grown like eight inches since I left."

She giggled, her eyes shining. "No, Dani! I'm the same size, you silly goose."

"Must be the camera angle then." I shrugged as my brother laughed in the background.

"We wanted to call and say hi and see how you were doing." His familiar face made my heart swell.

"Good, training is incredible here. This feels like a community of people I could really settle into, you know?" This was the feeling I had been missing from my previous company. A sense of rightness, a puzzle piece gently snuggled in with the rest of them.

"I'm glad to hear it. What are you working on right now?" he asked as Lily hummed on the floor next to him, playing with some toy truck.

"We have a lot of fluffy gigs, like corporate events, where I just get to float around and practice my music. Sometimes, I hop up on some apparatuses for ambient performance, but these types of gigs pay way better than anything else I've done." Shows were amazing because you got to work long and hard to perfect your craft. Ambient corporate gigs were great to explore and be weird, but not as fulfilling as something you poured your heart and soul into.

"Ah, we like it when the money is good," Soaren said.

"Yeah. They also have several resident shows lined up, and I'm really excited for them. It feels collaborative, like they want my input and my ideas. It's truly incredible..." I trailed off, not knowing how to bring up the living situation since this was my brother's doing, and I was really grateful, but it just wasn't ideal for me forever.

"Why do I feel like there is a *but* coming along?" He lifted his eyebrows at me as Lily did a little dance behind him.

I giggled. "Well, I'm really appreciative of this living situation with your friends. I'm just eager to find something else that feels more like what I need."

"Do you need help paying for a place, Dani?" He turned on that big-brother voice where he was trying to act like a dad.

"Not right now. I think it's just hard for me to wrap my head around paying for a studio by myself. I'm going to see if anyone at Cirque Callisto knows of anyone who needs a roomie. I'd like to live with other people, and the idea of having a random roommate kind of gives me anxiety, but I'll figure it out." I tugged on my ear absentmindedly, and Soaren gave me a look like he knew this was spiking my nerves.

"The offer still stands regardless. I know this isn't ideal. You would rather live with people who are your friends than your boring older brother's college roommate."

"I don't think you're boring!"

"Daddy is boring!" Lily sang in the background, which got laughs from both of us.

"I'll keep you posted if I need more help. You've already given me a ton of money and more to move here. I don't want to take advantage of that." There was a troublesome sensation in the back of my mind with the amount of financial help my brother had given me throughout our adult lives. He would never ask for anything in return, but it was still hard for me to receive it nonetheless.

"Dani, you and Lily are it. You're my people. I would happily give you all the money you need. You've helped me more than you will ever know, and I will always be grateful." Tears shined in his eyes. He was right, though. We loved our grandparents, but they were off living their retired lives and checking in when they could. But the three of us were a team. We supported one another no matter what.

"Don't you start this, because I'm going to start crying." Grabbing a tissue, I swiped at my eyes.

"Dani is the best," Lily agreed from where she was dancing along to the TV in the background.

"That she is, darling," Soaren mused.

"Tell me, what's new with you two?" I wanted to get this

conversation off the track of Soaren sending me more money. Lily was a beautiful and easy distraction.

"Lily, want to tell Dani what you did on the playground today?" Soaren asked, and her face lit up.

"I swung on the monkey bars! Just like you, Dani!" She danced around and clapped her hands.

"Holy cow! That's amazing, Lily Bug!" I rolled over onto my side and snuggled my head against my bicep. "What else did you do?" I asked.

She proceeded to prattle on about the slide, the swings, and all the other adventures that only kids could find on the playground until it was time for her to go to bed.

"Don't be a stranger, Dani. Text or call if you need anything, and tell me when you have some show dates, okay?" Soaren would want to come visit as soon as I told him it was okay, I just wasn't sure when that would be.

"You got it. Love you."

"Love you too." Soaren waved and Lily blew kisses before they hung up.

I was never interested in having kids, but I would light the world on fire for that little girl. It was one of the reasons I wanted private lessons for kids who needed help with their music journey. Just another reason why another living situation might be more ideal for all the things I wanted to do. I could have students come to me instead of me going to their houses.

But I needed a house for that, because apartments were pretty much a guaranteed noise complaint if I played for too long or too loud. Children who were just beginning were especially hard on the ears, and for that reason I could understand their frustrations.

Slowly, I worked on my website to build out what I would need to book private lessons for kids under a variety of instruments. The flute was my true love, but I could also play several other instruments well enough to help kids get started.

I wouldn't let that part of my website go live until I had a better place to live. Maybe I could rent out the Cirque Callisto studio space to hold lessons? I sent Logan an email asking about it.

If I could get just a few music students, then I could for sure feel more comfortable affording something else. And if I could have lessons at our studio, then I wouldn't need to look at renting a house; I could totally do an apartment.

God, why hadn't I thought of this idea sooner? The money I had saved up seemed to be going much quicker than I'd anticipated. But maybe that was my financial insecurities popping up.

Logan's reply came within minutes, and I wondered if she ever took a break. She said it would be totally fine and to just let her know the times so we could coordinate schedules, as Myla usually did silk privates during the days for a few clients.

I swallowed at that. Myla was a bit of an enigma to me. First off, from what I'd gathered, she was with some dumb-ass guy who couldn't be bothered to support her art form, which was obviously upsetting to her, but she refused to talk about it at length.

You could tell Logan, Jess, and Aven were bothered by it as well since they were her best friends. Why she was with someone like that, I had no idea. She was beautiful, smart, and strong. She deserved to be with someone who actually appreciated her as opposed to some piece-of-shit guy.

Hell, I would love to give him a piece of my mind.

I had a hard time not staring sometimes when she practiced at the studio. The way she moved on the silks was like a poetic dance. It was absolutely enthralling and captivating to watch her body sway with the music.

She had a true gift for this art form, and it was a shame she had a partner who couldn't see or respect that.

Men were the fucking worst, which was exactly why I stuck to femmes, other enbys, and trans folks. That, and I also wasn't attracted to men at all, thus the easiest thing for me was to stay the fuck away.

On that note, I decided to use my newly ignited rage at the patriarchy to make a game-time decision and post to my website that I was now available for private music lessons. Now, I could start getting a little more cash and feel more comfortable looking for a new place.

One press of the button, and I made it official. I closed my laptop and mentally applauded myself. I was a badass enby who did really cool shit. The patriarchy could go fuck itself, just like Myla's shitty boyfriend.

FIVE
MYLA: PRESENT DAY

I looked up at my ceiling and tried to will my body to rise. I didn't want to go out there and face him. Worst-case scenario, he wasn't moving his butt at all, and best-case scenario, he was already gone. The confidence I'd had last night was totally depleted, and I wanted to hide underneath my covers.

I knew the best I could hope for from Jake was sluggish movement indicating he was packing his stuff up. Additionally, he needed to get into the bedroom and grab some of his things anyway, so it wasn't the most realistic idea that he would have all his belongings out by the time I woke up. But it had made me feel powerful and strong and a little dramatic to tell him he needed to be out before I got up.

If only it could have really been that easy. A girl could dream.

Either way, he would need to be gone today. One way or another, he had to get the heck out of here. Sighing, I made myself get up and get dressed. I could do this. I just needed to put on my big-girl panties and face him. Where was that fierce, strong, and powerful woman from last night?

Exhausted, and in need of rest in between now and the next big battle.

Like a coward, I peeked my head out my door and heard him snoring away on the couch. Of course he was still here like nothing had happened last night. There was no sense of urgency, ever, in that man; not sure why I thought I could shove him into some last night.

"Are you kidding me?" My blood boiled with rage as I tried to take a few calming breaths to go out and tell him he had to get moving. What if I dumped a bucket of cold water on his face? Would that be too much? The longer he slept, the longer he was living here, and I could not have that anymore. Sleeping beauty would need to get his butt up.

I marched right out there and stared down at his sleeping form. Jake was attractive in a conventional beauty standard sort of way, but right now I wanted to strangle him and never see him again. He was negligent and disengaged. My eyes drifted to a pillow thrown on the floor. What if I whacked him upside the head with it? Or shoved it down on his stupid face and waited for him to turn blue?

Ugh, these were not the type of thoughts you had about someone you wanted to spend the rest of your life with. I tried to remember the last time I didn't have thoughts like this about him. Months? Years? Who could say.

Christ, I was over it.

"Jake." I tried to keep my voice even as he continued to snore away. He didn't even stir. The pillow was looking like a really good option right now.

"Jake." A little louder this time. Still nothing from his hulking form. Just one little slap with the pillow wouldn't really hurt him, right? I was sure it would barely make a dent on his dumb, handsome face.

"JAKE," I screamed, and he startled awake.

"Myla, what the fuck?" He scratched at his head like he

couldn't possibly fathom why I'd woken him up in such a violent manner. I should have chosen the pillow option.

"You're supposed to be on your way out the door," I said, channeling the Myla from last night. The one who could say what she wanted and mean it. Crossing my arms in front of me, I tried to exude power and confidence. Even though my hands were shaking. This was even worse than last night. My prowess was nonexistent this morning, and I really needed to cry for an emotional release. Why was I the one who wanted to flee when it was my house?

"You really thought I would be up and out at the ass crack of dawn?" He looked at me like I was joking. Unfortunately, I was not. Also, I didn't believe you could really categorize nine in the morning as the "ass crack of dawn". But whatever.

"I at least expected you to have the decency of trying to get your stuff out of here. I'm serious, Jake. We're over, and you need to get out. Today." I stomped my foot for emphasis and immediately felt like a child, but I was taking what I could get here.

"And how am I supposed to do that?" He looked at me and rolled his eyes. I saw red and had to breathe out aggressively. It really was like arguing with a five-year-old.

"I don't know, Jake, but you have been here long enough, and I need you to get the heck out of my house!" I threw my hands up in the air and clenched my teeth.

"How about this... How about I go out for a few hours. I'll buy the groceries this time, and then we can talk about it some more." He was trying to placate me, and damn it, it made me even more pissed off. I could basically hear my teeth cracking from how hard I was clenching. I needed a new action plan. Two could play this little manipulation game.

"You know what? You're right. Let's just take a breather here. Go out for a few hours and then come back. We can have lunch together and talk this out more." I forced a smile and balled up my hands, digging my fingernails into the soft skin there. Playing fair was not working; I would need to play dirty with him. He'd backed me into a corner, and I was determined to not let him win this one.

"See, you just needed a little time to cool down." Jake gave me a pitying look like I just needed to meditate my problems away and then I would be okay with his behavior.

"Okay, I'll see you in a few hours then." I hustled back to my room and texted my people that they needed to be here within thirty minutes to get Jake the heck out. With the right numbers, we could get his stuff out of here ASAP. My window of opportunity was closing, but we could do this. *I* could do this.

I pressed my ear to my door until I heard him leaving, then busted out of there like a feral cat.

My people were on their way, and I would start to make some headway before they got here. I started throwing his garbage out of my closet and into the hallway. None of his things would ever be in this room *ever* again. He didn't deserve a nice, organized move. Instead, he would get a chaotic mess of boxes. He should consider himself lucky I didn't just dump it all out on the grass.

Digging through my storage, I found what I could to transport his stuff and just started tossing his crap in. It was honestly more than he would have done for me, but here we were nonetheless. Slowly, my crew came and with each one of them, I felt a little lighter.

"Thank you all for coming." I looked around at my old friends—Aven, Logan, and Jess. Plus my new friends—Bex, Dani, and Ozzie. Ugh, poor Bex, we had only met me like once, yet here he was rushing in to help. I wouldn't have necessarily included them, but Logan said she would bring the troops and apparently that was them.

"Let's get him the heck out," I said, and they all nodded in silence.

We all went to work, taking turns placing his things on the street, and I felt like I was floating away from the earth. Like gravity had been turned off and I was doing my best not to trip over my unattached feet. To say I felt out of my mind was an understatement, but I had been pushed to the extreme. Retaliation was needed, and if I had to look at his things sitting in my house for one more minute, I might burn my whole house down.

"You good?" Logan slid in next to me as I stood in the kitchen taking it all in.

"No, but I will be." Pressure ballooned in my chest, and I didn't know how it would pop. Crying. Screaming. Breaking things. I wasn't sure, but at some point something would need to give.

She squeezed me in a tight hug, then went back to work.

Finally, Jake came back, and I felt like I blacked out. Fragments pierced my memory like shards of glass. His anger and disbelief. My friends going to bat for me. A moment when I'd told Dani they could move in.

It all felt odd and disjointed in my head. Like a funny memory, something that played out like a movie I was watching but not really there. It made me unsure of what was real and what seemed like a dream.

It all happened too fast and too slow. My mind was like scrambled eggs, and my body felt impossibly foreign and heavy. All I knew was he left with everything he owned and minimal physical damage. My heart had broken a long time ago for him, and this was the first step in my healing journey.

"Myla, do you want to sit down?" Aven stood next to me, and I had no idea how long she had been trying to talk to me or how long I had been standing there watching the scene with Jake play out. Had he even spoken to me? Had I spoken to him? I couldn't remember even though it was moments ago. There was only Jess, Aven, and Logan in front of me. When had everyone else left?

Fuck.

"Sure." She led me over to the couch, where Jess was already ready with a glass of wine and Logan had a full bag of popcorn.

"Do you want to talk about it?" Jess asked.

"No," I murmured.

"Okay then, we'll just sit and eat and drink and watch a feel-good movie. What do you want to watch, Myla?" Aven asked.

"Maybe like a Disney movie or something?"

"*Hercules*?" Logan offered.

I nodded, and we all piled in together as a little cuddle puddle.

Well, this had been a weird day. Moments of it slammed into my brain randomly. How furious Jake was when I'd told him he had to get out. His face getting so aggressively red I'd thought he might pop a vein or something. But he'd needed to leave. We had been growing apart for months now, and it was time to just pull the plug. He couldn't hang out at my house any longer or I would have actually combusted. Everything he did set my nerves on fire, and I had been ready to throttle him if he'd stayed a second longer.

Thank god everyone had been able to come over and move everything out at lightning speed. Eventually the movie ended, and the girls left. They'd lingered, though, asking if I needed anything else, but I told them I would be fine.

And I would be fine.

But maybe not tonight. Tonight would be rough.

So now I was alone with my thoughts and a weird emptiness in my house. Like a ghost, I walked the rooms where Jake had inhabited. Holes where his stuff had been littered my place, and it didn't feel good or bad. It just was just a new normal to get used to.

But Dani would be moving in, and that would help. I remembered asking them in a frenzied panic, or, at least, that's what it had felt like. Or maybe they'd offered? I couldn't even remember; today had been such a mess of things. They were nice and kind, so surely it was the right choice? I wasn't sure of any of my choices anymore these days.

God, if I had to be alone in here with my thoughts and feelings for an extended period of time, I think I would lose it. The vacancy of his things felt odd, and somehow I ended up looking at my bed with my lips pursed.

Should I sleep in the bed we'd shared together? Jake had been on the couch for awhile, but we'd done things in this bed... The thought of sleeping in it made my skin crawl, but I couldn't afford to buy a brand-new mattress right now.

Maybe I could be on the couch instead? Jake wasn't even here anymore and he was still messing with my life. Dani would think I was an absolute weirdo for refusing to sleep here. I would worry about how I would handle that when they got here.

Slowly, I took in the rest of the disarray around me and decided the bed was the only thing giving me the heebie-jeebies. Maybe I could get a cheaper mattress off Facebook Marketplace or from goodwill? Oddly, that also didn't make me feel better. The idea of sleeping on someone else's mattress was not my favorite option.

"Ugh," I muttered, sitting on my couch and exhaling slowly. Thank god we hadn't merged finances yet. It had been on my mind before shit hit the fan, and I was glad I had never brought it up.

So many mistakes and red flags littered our journey over the last several years, and I had just ignored them all for the sake of Jake being hot and fun and easygoing.

Men sucked. And it felt like, at this moment, I did too, because I'd just let it happen.

I took a long, hot shower, hoping to wash off some of this strange day, then found my comfiest pajamas. Dani would be here soon, and all I had to do was make it through a couple nights until they got here.

I could do that, right?

This was my house, and I got to live here because I was the responsible one. The one who saved and built equity and did all that finance stuff. Who paid the whole freaking mortgage and did adult shit because I didn't have anyone else to just do it for me. My parents would of course help me out, but I was proud of what I'd built here. The idea of asking them for help felt weirdly like a failure, and I was doing my best to stand on my own two feet.

And sometimes being an adult meant ending things and calling it quits when it had run its course. Being an adult was exhausting, though. Today, I was not having fun with this whole grown-up thing.

I just had to make it one night at a time until Dani got here. They would make everything a little less awful. At least that's what I told myself again and again until I fell asleep.

Six

My entire life was littered around me. I didn't have much except my bedroom furniture. The rest of the place had obviously already been furnished when I moved in since Ashley and Mark had been here for quite some time. I slowly started putting clothes in bags and boxes. It wasn't much, but it was what I had.

My most precious possessions were my instruments, which I lovingly put away in their regular travel cases and started to find spots for among my growing piles of things. I would protect these with my life. Everything else was replaceable, but these were my treasures.

My mind kept flashing back to how furious Jake had been about having his junk pushed to the curb. Which was understandable and not unwarranted, except he had refused to leave, so that's the consequence he got. It was Myla's house, and he had basically just been a freeloader at that point. The whole thing felt like a bad rom-com moment. It was wild to me that he hadn't understood why he was kicked out even though it felt pretty obvious to the rest of us.

He'd needed to leave, and Myla had reached her breaking point.

Myla had seemed like a shell of herself when we'd all gotten there. She'd put on a brave face as we all went to work, but I could see that it was heavy for her. All I wanted was to wrap her up in my arms and stroke her hair, telling her I knew everything sucked right now, but it would eventually suck less.

Breakups were never easy, especially when you lived together. It was chaotic and messy and heart-wrenching. Hopefully it had been a little easier to have all of us there today. There was no way she could have done all that by herself in just a few hours.

I'd had my fair share of relationships, but none that ended like that. I had never gotten to the point where I'd lived with anyone, so I couldn't imagine what was going through her head right now.

Selfishly, I was glad Jake was gone. Living with her was a fantastic solution for my current situation. I only hoped she would feel the same way in a few days after the initial breakup haze cleared and she was settled into this new norm.

Her nerves were probably fried, and she was most definitely in shock. The way she had looked at me when the idea of living together came up... It had reached into my soul and tugged viciously. Her face looked genuinely hopeful and desperate, like she couldn't imagine what her next step would be but, goddamn, she would fight to get there. Myla could count on me to be a good friend and roommate. My inner overachiever wanted to help her through this tough spot and come out victorious on the other side.

There was a knock on my door, which caused me to jump. My door was almost always closed since I had tried to make myself as small as possible living here. Ashley and Mark never said anything, but it was just a general aura of discomfort, like they were fine to have me here but it would be better if I weren't. I did my best not to be a burden even though I always sort of felt like one.

"Dani?" Ashley's voice rang out from the other side. Telling them I was moving out had been easy. They had acted mildly surprised yet delighted that I had found some friends to settle in with. This was always meant to be temporary, and I would be lying if I said I wasn't itching to leave this behind.

They didn't ask for the details of my move, and I didn't provide them. Our relationship was politely uninterested at best. Which was fine. They were my brother's friends, not mine.

"Coming!" I got up and headed to the door. "What's up, Ashley?"

Ashley's long, blonde hair was in a high ponytail, and she wore leggings, an oversized sweatshirt, and Uggs. She pushed her glasses up on the bridge of her nose and gave me a warm smile.

"I just wanted to see if you needed any help with anything," she said.

"That's very sweet of you to offer, but I think I'm good. I didn't do a ton of unpacking anyway," I confessed.

Ashley nodded, but lingered like she wanted to say something else.

"I hope we didn't shove you out or anything," Ashley said, twisting her fingertips together.

"Not at all. I know this wasn't permanent for everyone, and I appreciate you letting me stay here while I was in transition. Maybe you all can come to one of my shows sometime?" I replied. It was the best I could think to offer up at this moment. We wouldn't hang out, and I didn't like to say things I didn't mean, but I was always happy to share what I did with people.

Ashley nodded. "Okay, sounds good. Just let me know if you need anything. I'm happy to help."

She walked away, and I shut the door. I wondered idealistically if she was looking for a friend in me. Adult friendships were hard, and maybe if things had been different we could have been pals. But where I needed to be was with Myla, not here.

I went back to collecting my things, and it only took an hour or two to get the rest of my stuff packed. There would be a few things to leave out since I had several more days here, but for the most part, I was ready to go.

My brother had texted me saying he wanted to chat about my new roomie situation, and I asked if now was a good time.

While I waited for his reply, I found myself wandering onto Myla's Instagram. I had been doing that a lot lately—watching her videos and looking at her performances. My mind could simply not wrap around how Jake had been such a dickhead about her art. It honestly was disgusting he didn't support her dreams. The sense of entitlement he had to her place, her time, and their relationship was astounding.

Clearly I had been team Myla all along. Scrolling through her Instagram, I nosily looked through the comments on her posts. Myla had a beloved following on social media. She was great at TikTok and Instagram, sharing her performances and goofy moments at Cirque Callisto. I found myself in a deep hole of reading comments about how people adored her and thought she was beautiful and talented.

She tried to reply to every single one, and it was obvious to see she appreciated everything these people were providing her. How could Jake be dense enough to think he didn't need to try? That he didn't have it so good to have someone like Myla as a partner?

He truly was the epitome of a man doing straight, dumb,

white-guy shit. It was easy enough to find his social media handles, and it was as dull and boring as I imagined him to be.

Myla's vibrance outshone him a million times over from what I could see. Not that social media gave the whole picture, but from what I knew from the team at Cirque Callisto, Myla, and this... He paled in comparison to her.

It seemed sometimes that was the curse of the patriarchy: Men doing the least and everyone else having to do the absolute most. It made my blood boil just thinking about it, so it was perfect timing when Soaren said he was ready to talk.

I FaceTimed him to see Lily's and his faces. They were my comfort people, and I missed them with my whole heart. I wished I could just transplant them here, or maybe Cirque Callisto there. Either way, that would be my perfect scenario.

"DANI!" Lily squealed into the phone and got her little nose right up in the camera.

"Lily! What are you up to on this fine day?" I lay back on my bed and snuggled in.

"Daddy and I were doing some finger painting. Look!" She ran with the phone, the picture getting blurry, before she halted in front of what looked like a day outside with the sun and flowers and three little stick people.

"Whoa! That's cool. Tell me more about your picture, Lily Bug."

"This is the sun, some flowers, and you and me and Daddy." She looked at it proudly, and it made my heart burst.

"Thanks for putting me in your picture." I would not cry on the phone with her despite her little voice making my heart sing.

"I miss you, Dani, but Daddy says you are following your dreams and it's important you do it," she said matter-of-factly, and the tears threatened to fall down my cheeks even more.

"That's very nice of you to say, Lily. I will come visit soon, or you can come here? Remember, we can FaceTime anytime, okay? I am never too busy for you," I said and absolutely meant it. Most of the time, I would stop whatever I was doing to get to chat with this little squirt.

She blew me a kiss, and Soaren appeared in the picture.

"Where's your picture?" I teased, and Soaren grinned and held up his own finger-painting masterpiece. It looked like some sort of animal. A cat or a dog?

"I know it's incredibly obvious, but it's a cow!" He grinned, and I giggled.

"Daddy says all the art went to you." Lily giggled too.

"I'm not great at finger painting, but I can play music and I can move my body." I did a little shimmy, and Lily joined in as we shook our shoulders and laughed.

"Lily, why don't you go grab your jammies while I talk to Dani for a minute." He ruffled her hair, and she sped off, blowing kisses at me.

"God, I miss her. I mean, I miss you too, but she is the greatest little thing," I mused.

"Isn't she, though? All the good parts of me and all the good parts of Millie." He looked at where she ran off, and it radiated love and care.

"How are you holding up? I miss you both. I wish I could just squish you two and my circus together in one place." I pulled on my ear idly.

"We miss you too. We're always closer than you think. We're good. Same old, same old here. Tell me about your new roommate!" He wasted no time getting to the point.

"Her name is Myla, and..." I gave him the whole rundown of what happened—how Jake was a massive asshole and Myla was amazing, talented, and beautiful and truly deserved more from him—and it was a miracle I didn't go punch him in the face right now as I was rehashing the whole story.

"Wow, okay, I'm glad she's okay. That sounds horrible."

"Yeah, she's just amazing, and I can't imagine why anyone

would not be interested in what she does or support her craft, because it's truly breathtaking and poetry in the air," I said wistfully. I couldn't wait to see her perform more. The way she made people feel when she performed was nothing short of magical.

"Dani?" Soaren said, looking at me skeptically.

"What?"

"Do you have a crush on Myla?"

The question slammed into my body like a ton of bricks. "What?! No! Why would you say that?" I was an adult. Crushes were for teenagers and middle schoolers. Anytime I had a crush as a child, it was disastrous. The fumbled kisses and misread signals led to unnecessary drama because we were all navigating horny feelings for the first time.

"You're talking about her like she is the greatest and most beautiful person you have ever seen." He quirked a brow up at me.

"She is!" I said, realizing maybe I *did* feel something for her. "What if I do?" This was bad. This was very, very bad. How did I not realize this sooner? I had just agreed to live with her, and now here I was being super creepy and infatuated with her. It was like the horror of thirteen-year-old me all over again when I fell in love with my best friend, who was most certainly not into me and as straight as could be. When I'd confessed my feelings to her, that had been the end of the friendship.

"Dani, it's fine. Take a deep breath," Soaren commanded, and I obeyed.

"That is really creepy!" I flailed my arms about, as if I could get rid of this feeling by shaking it off my bones. The anxiety skittering across my skin felt like a million little bugs trying to burrow into my body. I could not do this. I would need to call this whole thing off.

"You're not a kid anymore. What happened with Olivia is

different. It will be okay; you know how to be an appropriate adult with boundaries, and who knows, maybe she has a crush on you too," he said casually. I nearly lost it right then and there. *How was he that calm about this?*

The memory of me giving Olivia a bracelet I'd made and confessing my feelings flooded my mind. She had run out of our house and flung the bracelet at my head. Soaren had been right there to witness it all. He had held me as I sobbed because Olivia was everything to me in that moment, and she never spoke to me again. In fact, her family had moved away shortly after.

High school had gotten better, but I'd made a rule to not fall in love with any more friends. It was too vulnerable, yet here I was making the same mistakes from my youth. My skin felt too hot, and sweat pooled in my armpits. This was a bad idea. A very bad idea. Was it too late to bail out now? God, what was worse? Disappointing Myla because she was counting on me to move in with her or living with her and silently lusting after her?

"What did I just get myself into?" My chest was rising and falling rapidly. A deep sense of fight or flight flooded my body, and I closed my eyes to try and collect myself.

"Dani, I know memories of the past are telling you this will be the same. But it won't be. This is different. *You* are different. What if you just took it day by day instead of picturing the demise of this situation?" Soaren asked.

"You're right. I'm being irrational. I guess I didn't realize what these feelings were until you rudely pointed them out," I said, scowling at him, and he had the audacity to chuckle.

"You'll figure this out. In the meantime, I can't wait to see how this pans out." Soaren smirked, and I glared at him.

Now that my crush was out in the open, I needed to get it under control. It was like a celebrity crush. Harmless, really. Nothing would ever come of it, so you just allowed it to exist and didn't give it too much attention. That's all. I wasn't going to do anything because Myla needed a friend and a roomie, which was exactly what I would be.

There would be no tomfoolery on my part, and living with her would probably desensitize me to thinking she was wonderful. She probably did tons of weird, unattractive stuff in her own home that would ultimately help me get over this.

This would be fine. I was sure of it.

A little crush wouldn't tear this whole thing down. I would just let it fizzle out. No reason to drag up demons from my past. This was something I could handle, no problem. Easy peasy.

SEVEN

MYLA

My home felt different. Not bad, but not good. *Yet.* Just forever changed. It was a complicated emotional ball weighing heavy in my chest. My relationship with Jake had really ended months ago, yet I didn't have the words to tell him it was over until now. Sighing, I thought maybe I should also get a pet? A kitten or puppy could be nice. I wondered if Dani had any experience with animals and could help.

The thought of truly being alone made me want to crawl out of my skin. If left to my own devices, I thought I might spontaneously combust. I'd known Jake had to go, but I didn't know how uncomfortable I was when it was just me and my thoughts. My feelings bounced around my head like ping-pong balls, and I struggled to keep my composure.

It wasn't like I didn't know how to be alone or that I didn't enjoy my company. Half of being an adult was being okay with not having people around you all the time, but I felt haunted. As if my brain couldn't get out of this hamster wheel of emotions. Sitting and thinking through my thoughts over and over again was actually the complete opposite of helpful.

My mind was sucking me into a descent to madness, and I absolutely needed some distractions to claw my way out of this spiral.

Thank god Dani agreed to live here. They would be here tomorrow, and it would feel less weird in this house with their calming energy, I was sure. Unlike my other friends, Dani hadn't said much about what they thought about my relationship with Jake. Granted, they had only been here a little bit, while Logan, Jess, and Aven had been by my side for years. But I appreciated their presence, nonetheless. Jess, Logan, and Aven were battle-ready at any point to defend me against Jake, while Dani was more interested in hearing what I wanted and how I preferred to deal with him.

Dani always seemed to want to soothe, as opposed to everyone else who were ready to rip Jake a new asshole. Both energies were necessary, but not all the time. Especially now that Jake was gone, I needed someone who would just be here —no judgment or shame, just exist with me in a way that made me feel like I wasn't losing my mind all the time. Because I'd really had no idea how loud my head was going to be until right freaking now. It was overwhelming, and I really needed the voices in my head to shut the hell up for a second so I could think straight.

Tonight, it was just me, though. One more night. One more night of this uncomfortable solitude, and then it would be over. At least for a little while. I could do this. I was a goddamn independent woman who didn't need a man. This was my house. I had a master's degree, and I could fly through the air, doing incredible physical feats people could only dream of accomplishing. I could exist in my home, by myself, after this horrendous break up. Sleeping in this space by myself was absolutely something I could do. I sat on my couch and looked around, feeling the silence settle in my bones.

"Music. I need music to make the thoughts in my head less

loud," I murmured as I hustled around to set up my speaker and a playlist. Soft notes began playing, and my shoulders pulled away from my ears. This was good. Progress.

I stripped off my clothes and slid my pajamas on. But I was stuck looking at my bed. Our bed, really. A beautiful king-sized mattress with a pillow top that made you feel like you were floating on clouds. Except I still couldn't sleep there.

Even though it had been months since Jake and I had been in that bed together, I couldn't get myself to lay down in it now that he was gone. What was wrong with me? I'd bought the bed. The bed was, in all ways, mine, not his. I should be able to reclaim this thing and mark my territory. I had been doing this weird song and dance with the bed since Jake had left. It was horrendously embarrassing, but the idea of laying my body down there and trying to fall asleep seemed actually inconceivable.

Images of us sleeping together and having sex in that bed flashed into my mind, and they sort of made me want to throw up. Fine. I would try sleeping in the bed tomorrow night. This standoff could not last forever, and I would eventually get to the point where I could sleep on this dumb mattress. It had only been a few days, but I would warm up to the idea. There was no rush to make up with my beautiful bed. It would still be there tomorrow.

That meant I could sleep on the couch, which is where Jake had slept for the past several months. But whenever I looked at the couch, I felt nothing. Running back to my room, I lay down on the bed, and a wave of nausea hit me again.

"No, no, no, noooo."

The symbolism of the bed was messing with my head. Maybe this problem wouldn't go away. Would I seriously need to get a new mattress? The thought of that seemed wildly absurd, but I wasn't sure I had another answer. Why did I have to fork over a thousand or so dollars for a new mattress because the idea of sleeping in this one made me want to gag?

Get it together, Myla.

I was pissed at Jake and at myself. Why did the stupid bed have to be my breaking point?

Grumbling, I set myself up on the couch with the music to ease the tension in my body. Sighing, I lay down and got on my phone. First, I started out on a pet adoption website, because I, for sure, needed a pet. An animal was scientifically proven to reduce anxiety and stress. This would be the perfect post-breakup choice. Pets loved you unconditionally and snuggled you when you were sad and wiggled and cuddled when you were happy. This was an excellent idea. I would consult with Dani about it when they got here, since they would also be living here, but I couldn't imagine it would be a problem.

Scrunching my brows, I wondered if this was too rash. Was it too soon to get a break-up pet? I just wanted something to fill this uncomfortable void in my chest. Obviously, I was glad to be rid of him, but he'd still left a huge hole behind. One that seemed to ooze and ache at my breastbone. Screw Jake and his stupid, obnoxious face.

I sent Dani a quick text asking how they felt about a dog or a cat. But maybe we could be, like, hedgehog people or something? Would that be weird? Or a ferret? I didn't know, just another living creature to care for sounded nice.

When I finally convinced myself I shouldn't get too attached to anything before I heard from Dani, I decided to scroll on Instagram, and what did I find? An ad for a dating app popped up. It was like the universe knew I was now single and wanted me to get back out there.

Ugh, the internet was a scary place. But maybe this was the sign I needed. Wasn't it Dua Lipa who had said the best way to get over someone was to get under someone else? I hadn't been laid in months, and it sounded like a productive way to celebrate my new single era.

"You know what? I can date. This will be good for me." Quickly, I downloaded a few apps and began the egregious process of filling out my dating profiles.

Was dating in your thirties better or worse than dating in your twenties? I really had no idea. As a newly identified queer woman, how the heck was I supposed to figure out how to date other people besides men?

It was fine. I could figure this out. I went through my mental list of all my accomplishments again to prove to myself I could do hard things.

Slowly, I filled out all the funny question prompts that apparently were supposed to make you feel witty and cute, but made me feel silly and boring. Then the pictures and all the other random junk. Would people think I was showing off by posting circus and aerial pictures? Or maybe it would seem boring to only post pictures of me standing and smiling? Screw it, I would do a mix of both and go from there.

Finally, I got to the point of hitting publish on my multiple profiles and needed to decide how I identified and what I was looking for. I wanted to know what it was like to date people other than men. But I was terrified. All I knew and was comfortable with was dating straight guys. But they were kind of the worst, honestly, so it was time to expand my horizons.

"Your queer identity is valid, Myla. You can do this. Don't be a scaredy cat."

God, I had resorted to talking to myself regularly and giving myself little pep talks. Was this really all my future had in store for me?

Okay, back to the stupid profile. I said I was interested in men, women, enbys, and trans and queer folks alike. I was half tempted to ditch men altogether. But what about all the queer men? I would definitely be interested in them, so I guess the categories would stay. This was a great first step. Mentally, I high-fived myself. *Woohoooo. Myla for the win.*

"No swiping tonight. You did the hard part of just getting started." I mentally patted myself on the back and allowed my heavy body to sink into the pillows.

Okay, I could do this. My phone dinged, and it was Dani.

> **Dani: I love all animals! A puppy or kitty**
> **would be great. I would love to help**
> **you care for them too. :)**

I smiled and went to reply almost instantly. See? Things were already going better than expected. Soon there would be Dani, some pets, and maybe a new partner in the mix. Things were definitely going in the right direction. I just had to relax and let it happen.

> **Me: Thank god. I need some noise and**
> **chaos in this house to quiet my brain.**
> **Maybe they will help me fill this gaping**
> **wound in my chest. It probably couldn't**
> **hurt, right? And with the two of us, we**
> **should be able to tackle it no problem.**

I hit send, then a wave of anxiety hit me. Was that too much information? I didn't want to burden anyone else with the ache in my bones right now. I picked at my nails absent-mindedly, waiting for them to reply. Crap, they probably didn't want to move in now because I was a hot post-breakup mess. My emotions went from flying high and looking at all the positives to taking a nose dive straight into Negative Nelly town and splatting unceremoniously on the ground.

> **Dani: I've heard kitties and puppies help
> heal just about anything. Should we
> head to the local shelters sometime
> soon and see what they have?**

Breathing a sigh of relief, I replied back. I needed to get this pendulum swing of emotions under control before I had a heart attack.

> **Me: That sounds amazing. Thank you
> for agreeing to be my roommate and
> answering my unhinged text messages
> about adopting animals. I'm really
> grateful for you. Can't wait for you to
> be here tomorrow. Sweet dreams!**

Dani's words made me feel a little less worked up about everything. Things would look different tomorrow. Today just needed to end.

Okay, I could do this. Dani and I would make a great team. They were the exact type of friend and roommate that would make this easy-peasy.

I decided to give my bed one last go, which was actually a huge mistake as I walked in and immediately turned away, the sight of it making my stomach do flips.

"Heard loud and clear, body. The couch it is." Just one more night here. Tomorrow was surely the day I could sleep there, and I wouldn't have to get a new mattress. The idea was silly; I would overcome my fears of that bed if it was the last thing I did.

Maybe I needed to get a comfier couch if this were to be my fate. I tried my best to settle, but it felt like sleep was the last thing my body could do at the moment. I decided to get up and do some jumping jacks and dance around, but I felt like a weirdo running around my house.

Then I thought a snack would make me feel better. Or some tea. Neither one of those things did anything for me.

I just wanted to go to bed and wake up with a new day tomorrow. Maybe some melatonin would help? I took a few gummies, lay down on my couch, and simply waited for what felt like hours for the medicine to kick in.

My head kept swimming with thoughts of Jake's negligence in our relationship and my lack of communication in saying what I needed and wanted from him. The way I came out to him and how he treated it in such an underwhelming way, I thought I would cry.

Coming out later in life while in a hetero relationship was already a brain bender, let alone when your partner acted like it was the same as just telling him what you ate for lunch that day. It was a whole revelation of my identity and who I was and how I operated day to day. He had acted like it was a throw-away piece of information.

Slowly, my eyes felt heavy, and I prayed to whatever god existed out there that it would be a dreamless, peaceful sleep. Too bad whoever was out there didn't hear a damn thing.

I tossed and turned all night, haunted by the last several days of my life and how the hell I would operate moving forward.

EIGHT
DANI

The rain outside was absolutely relentless today, falling in thick sheets and covering everything in sight. It created a calming white noise that soothed my body and made me more excited to dive into training today. I was waiting for Logan to show up as there was a strict rule to train in the buddy system so in case anyone got hurt, someone else would be there to help. I began with gentle stretches and mobility movements. As I was starting to hang up my straps, Logan came through the door in a whirlwind.

"Jesus, it's a fucking swamp out there." She shook herself like a wet dog. But despite it being a monsoon outside, she came in looking her usual put-together self. Her long, pink hair was in a claw clip piled on top of her head, and she wore a matching workout set that showed off the expansive artwork on her skin. Logan was strong and lithe, confident and capable in the air and on the ground.

"I kind of like it," I said. There was something calming about Mother Nature taking control.

"All I want to do is curl up in a ball, watch a movie, and drink some tea. But alas, the circus must go on." She winked as she set her stuff down and pulled off her shoes. There seemed to always be shows and gigs going on, as well as our circus classes and school. Logan ran the whole thing like a fucking champ. I couldn't imagine what her schedule was like or all the things that were on her plate. She hardly ever complained, though—she seemed to genuinely love what she did, and I knew she loved her people with equal fierceness. But I sometimes wondered if she was overwhelmed. Surely she would ask for help if she needed it? It didn't feel like my place to push.

"Is anyone else coming in today?" I asked.

"Myla will be here, but I think some of the others might come in later. It depends on how long you're staying. I thought it might be a good chance for us to work out the private schedule." She strode over to the warehouse and put up her trapeze.

"She asked me if it would be okay for us to get a pet. Isn't that cute?" I mused, and Logan lifted one of her brows. Pets made everything better.

"A breakup puppy?"

"Or kitty." We hadn't decided on the details, but I could be persuaded either way. Pets got you in ways regular people didn't, and I would love to have a little critter running around.

"Very cute. You'll have to let me know if you end up getting one, because, of course, I will be the cool aunt." She smirked, and I giggled. As if Logan could be anything else but that.

Suddenly, the front door burst open to a feral-looking Myla. She had dark circles underneath her bloodshot brown eyes. Her normal dewy skin looked pale, and her dark-purple hair was sticking out in funny places. She looked like she hadn't been sleeping, or maybe she had been crying. My heart twisted in my chest. Maybe I should have called her instead of texting. Not that it was any of my business per se but I cared about Myla as a friend and my roomie.

Not to mention, she was soaked to the bone from the rain, as though she had been outside for hours rather than minutes. Droplets of water littered the ground around her, and she shuddered nervously like a scared animal.

"Are you... alright?" Logan's mouth dropped open in a little *o* as Myla stomped inside. Logan didn't ever mince her words, and she wouldn't usually let things go under the radar because her policy was to get it out in the open.

"No, I slept like absolute trash and it's pouring." She pouted.

"I mean you've had a big couple of days, Myla. Having trouble sleeping is normal after everything that's happened," I said softly. Logan nodded in agreement as she continued to scan Myla for any other obvious signs of distress.

"It was like my body couldn't figure it out. As if I haven't been sleeping like a normal human being my whole stupid life. All I wanted to do was sleep, but it's like my brain was a rat on a wheel, spinning and spinning. And while I had been mentally sprinting, the night had come and gone, which meant I needed to get my butt here." She looked dazed and out of sorts as she prattled on. I had the sudden urge to giggle uncomfortably. It wasn't funny, but her state of rumpledness was honestly adorable, and I just wanted to wrap her up like a burrito and lull her to bed. But I would just keep those thoughts to myself.

"Myla, you know my rules about training and sleep?" Logan poised it as a question we all already knew the answer to.

"I know. I'm not training today. Less than six good hours of sleep and we aren't allowed in the air," Myla repeated, sighing like she was truly disappointed in herself. As if her sleepless night was her fault and not a symptom of her current circumstances.

"From experience, I need at least eight good hours to have a safe training day, but six is the minimum. I had someone fall off a lyra once because she was exhausted. Not here, but at another training facility. Somebody has to look out for you all." She stood with her hands on hips like she meant serious business. I'd signed some waivers when I first got here, but I had forgotten that rule. It made sense, but I hadn't known how seriously things were enforced.

"Good to know you're taking care of us, Logan." I gave her a smile.

"Somebody has to." She grinned, the seriousness of the moment dissolving. I tried not to fidget as the tension eased.

"Can we talk about the private schedule thing you texted me about, Lo? Let's do that, then you two can train and I will just wallow in my wetness." Myla stripped off some layers as Logan tossed her a towel.

My mind went to something extremely inappropriate as small strips of Myla's skin were exposed, and I had to rein it in. My small, miniscule crush on Myla was a bad idea. She had just gotten out of a relationship with an idiotic man and we were going to be roommates. There was no place for romance here. Soaren's teasing tickled the edges of my consciousness, and I tried to push it away. This wasn't the time or place for thoughts like this. They would need to fuck off and find somewhere else to go.

"You wallow in whatever you need to, babes," Logan purred, and I giggled at that. It dragged a small grin from Myla's lips that warmed my belly.

"I don't think going to the animal shelter will work today either, Dani, considering the weather," Myla said sadly. I knew she wanted to get a pet, but I didn't realize the sense of urgency behind it.

"We have all the time in the world to find our perfect little creature." I winced at using the word *our*. Why did I do that? Myla seemed unbothered by it, but it made my skin crawl to make such a bold assumption.

Logan smacked her lips. "Aw, how sweet you two are already planning for your first child!" She clapped her hands excitedly.

That earned an eye roll from Myla. Wow, she was cute when she did that. Things were getting out of control in my mind when Myla started towel-drying her violet hair, and I had a flash of her fresh out of the shower. Jesus Christ, I was like a deranged, horny teenage boy.

"Anyway, I usually have privates during the day here, but I think Logan said yours was for music students, not aerial?" Myla tried to smooth down the flyaways around her face, but they just kept curling up, creating a halo of purple around her.

"Yeah, it's mostly... Are you okay with kids playing shitty music in here while you work with other clients? It's a bit challenging, because when kids are first learning something like a violin, it's painful to listen to for hours on end." Most people recognized that but didn't realize how bad it was until they were forced to listen to it for long periods of time. I secretly loved the evolution of screeching notes to beautiful melodies. The growth was extremely satisfying.

Logan winced at that, like it wasn't her favorite idea. I got the impression she was not a kid person.

"Ahh okay, I now understand our predicament." Myla plopped down on the ground and furrowed her brows, like she was thinking intently on what the solution could be.

"It's not a big deal. I don't have to take clients. I can look for a music space," I hurriedly said, not wanting to inconvenience anyone. But I did really like taking privates, and the money was always good.

"Okay, idea," Logan said slowly.

"Let's hear it." Myla looked at her eagerly.

"What if, Dani, you did lessons out of Myla's house since you will be living there anyway? Because it's not like you need anything special in terms of space, right? Whereas obviously for aerial we need the rigging and equipment. And Myla's neighbors aren't too close, so it could be perfect! Nobody's ears will bleed from those adorable little gremlins learning how to play." Logan looked pleased with this solution, and I had to admit it was a good one.

"No special equipment needed as they will be bringing their own instruments, and I already have my own, but it's your house, Myla. I don't want to encroach on your space or anything." It was a great idea, but I didn't know how Myla would feel about it.

"It sounds like my ears will be happier for it since I'll be here during the day most of the time anyway." Myla beamed, giving me a thumbs-up.

"Perfect! It's settled. Dani will start lessons out of your house, and then we can all refrain from wearing earplugs here," Logan mused.

"Is it really that bad when they start to learn?" Myla tugged on her hair.

"I'll record a little snippet and share with everyone. Imagine screeching from an animal being attacked... sort of like that." Grinning, I remembered when I'd first started play-ing, and Soaren would complain about the noise. Everyone had to be bad at first, it was just the way it was. Then the more you practiced, the more it turned into a full-fledged song.

"Thank you for your service." Logan saluted at me, and I snickered.

"Anything for the youths of tomorrow," I teased.

"Oh my god," Myla groaned.

"So you're grounded today, and the two of us will do our own thing. Got it, Myla?" Logan pointed her finger aggressively at her. Her take-no-shit attitude was back, and I couldn't even imagine going against what she said when she got like that.

"Yes, ma'am. Dani, do you need help moving your stuff?" Myla turned her attention to me fully, and I had to fight off the heat that crawled up my cheeks.

"Because you know we've got a team assembled and ready to go." Logan struck some superhero poses like she was part of the Justice League or something. We both chuckled as she slid down to the ground Black Wiidow style.

"I think I just need one other human, and Bex already offered. I was planning on coming later tonight with most of my things, if that's okay?" Bex and I had been fast friends since he was sort of new to this bunch as well, but we were both finding our spots in the community.

"Totally, I will be there." Myla gave me a thumbs-up.

"I cannot wait to get out of my current living situation, as it's not exactly ideal. They're my brother's friends and really nice, but I just feel like I'm a bit of a nuisance or inconvenience to them, you know?" I pulled at my ear. They had taken the news well when I'd told them I found a different solution for living. My plan was to get them a gift card and some chocolate and wine as a way to say thanks.

Ashley and I'd had that weird moment. I was probably making it out to be bigger in my head than it actually was. It was easy for me to think I was a burden to other people, even when logically I knew that wasn't the case, and we had all agreed on terms.

"Now you get to hang out with cooler people all the time." Myla waggled her eyebrows at me, and Logan did the same.

"The coolest," I said in fake awe. Giggles erupted in the room, and it felt good. Normal to be with these people in our space, just being ourselves.

"If you need more help, you know you can call me and I'll come over. Otherwise, I'm going to get in there and start my conditioning before I tackle my giant email inbox." Logan walked off, and I lingered for a minute as Myla got comfy doing some stretches on the floor.

"Thank you for letting me room with you. I'm way more grateful than you'll ever know." It had all happened very quickly. Half of me was worried Myla would change her mind since she went through such an intense breakup, but so far she had only seemed to be doubling down and investing even more in us as roommates.

"Dani, you're the one saving me. That house feels weird now, and I want it to feel like my home. Because it was just my house before Jake got there, and I want it to feel like my sanctuary once again. You being here feels like a step in the right direction." Myla propped her chin on her palm.

The blush was back as I nodded. "Either way, you rule and now I'm going to go tackle my straps act."

"Good luck!" Myla blew me a kiss, and I turned away, my cheeks on fire.

I definitely would need to get this under control. My attraction to Myla had no place in our relationship right now. For the next hour, I tried to ignore the butterflies in my belly and the warmth in my chest.

I kept playing her words over and over in my head. She needed me to help bring her some ease and peace. And damn, I would do my best to give her exactly that.

NINE

MYLA

I ended up wasting my whole day at the studio. Most of my private clients canceled due to the weather, which was a relentless onslaught outside. It wasn't my favorite day, but at least yesterday was over. My sleep had been absolutely terrible. I didn't know if it was a combination of the couch and an exhausting day yesterday or the anxiety rolling through my body. Probably my relationship detonating like a bomb, but there was nothing to do about it now, considering I was the one who lit the fuse. Either way, I would not be able to function on this level of sleep for more than a couple days.

The weather really put a cloud over my head as well. Dani had left to get their stuff. I offered once more to help, but they waved me off, saying they had it handled and that Bex was on his way already. Those two really had seemed to hit it off. I liked both of them a lot, and the more friendship in our community space, the better. Being the new artists in town could be hard, but I knew they would find their spots and get settled in no time.

Instead of doing anything productive, I continued to hang around the studio space and decided to look back at my dating profiles. The doomscroll took over for about an hour with incessant swiping until Logan stood over me.

"Myla, I've been calling your name for like the last ten minutes. You okay?" she asked, wiping sweat from her brow.

How long had I been zoned out?

"Why are you sweating? I thought you finished training a while ago." I looked at her closely. I couldn't tell if it was my imagination or not, but I could see the faintest hint of dark circles under her eyes.

"Stress sweat. All these emails are weighing on me. But I'll get through it. It's not the fun part of this, though," she said, her brows pinched together. Logan was notoriously bad at asking for help and leaning on others to delegate hard tasks. Checking in on her was hard, because she usually waved you away like it wasn't a big deal until she was breaking down on the floor. Even then, she liked to pretend everything was fine once her meltdown had happened; she just needed a release even though what she really needed was better support. I was about to dive further into what was weighing on her when Aven burst through the door.

"What's up, bitches!" Aven walked in, shaking her umbrella. "Why are you on the floor?"

"It grounds me." I stuck my tongue out at her, and she did the same. Logan's features seem to slide back into their cool confidence, but the beads of sweat still lingered.

"I get it. What's this about stress sweating, Lo?" Aven tied her curly black hair back in a little puff. Leave it to Aven to be persistent against Logan's walls.

"Emails," she grumbled.

"Do you need help with them?" Aven asked. She was the best at fighting against Logan even if it wasn't always pretty.

"Nope," Logan said, popping the *p*.

"Lo... ask for help when you need it," Aven warned, narrowing her eyes.

"I know. This isn't one of those times, but thank you." Logan's smile didn't have the same zest it normally did, but if she said she was fine, I guess she was fine. You couldn't help people who didn't want it.

"I got my eyes on you." Aven pointed her fingers from her own eyeballs to Logan's. Logan let out a breathy laugh.

"Anyway, I was calling out to Myla for several minutes, but she ignored me. She was very preoccupied with her phone." Logan's eyebrows were sky high as she zeroed her attention on me, and I nearly cursed. Logan was great at deflecting, and it landed right in my face.

"And what, pray tell, is profoundly interesting on your phone, my dear Myla?" Aven crossed her arms and looked down at me. She was exactly as perceptive as Logan was and could be just as pushy when she wanted to. Aven was a bit more selective, though, whereas Logan bulldozed through whatever she wanted.

"Nothing," I murmured, but before I knew what was happening, Aven had snatched my phone and looked at my dating profile. Cackling, she danced away from my hands and scanned the screen as Logan flew in behind her to get the same information.

"So you're putting yourself out there right away? Respect." Logan gave me a little round of applause.

"I mean, I couldn't sleep last night, so I did this instead. I've matched with a few people since I've been swiping for the last hour." Half of me wanted to throw my phone against the wall, and the other half wanted to be glued to the app. Ugh. Dating in any shape or form sucked some major balls.

"Let me see these matches." It was Logan's turn to grab the phone and scroll through. "These are all men."

"Is that what you want?" Aven asked. There was no judgment or shame. Just curiosity. Logan was the only one out of us who had a strong proclivity for men, which she claimed was her biggest downfall, but she was open to whatever human being came her way. I had discovered I leaned more toward masculinity, but not necessarily men.

"Not really. I have it set to everyone, but I keep getting only men fed to me. Sometimes there are women, but a lot of them say something along the lines of 'my husband is okay with a play thing' or 'I just want a friend'. Which is confusing, right? If I wanted to be a play thing, I feel like I would go somewhere else, and same if I just wanted a friend." I frowned. I thought online dating was supposed to make things easier for queer people. It honestly left me feeling dazed and unsure.

"That's why I'm on a dating-app hiatus." Aven shrugged. "Very straight forward if you know what I mean."

Giggling, I held out my hand for my phone. "Plus I don't know how to date outside of dudes very well. I think I just need to stretch my dating muscles with these dumb guys, then I'm ready to be a queer cutie, you know?" At least, that's what I kept telling myself. Women, enbys, trans folks, and other queer people alike sort of intimated me, especially when I thought about getting intimate. What if I was terrible in bed because I didn't know what was going on and then died of embarrassment?!

"Whatever you need to do, babes, is great. Proud of you for saying what you need and want." Logan plopped down beside me with a granola bar in hand. Aven joined us on the floor.

"So what did you need from me?" I asked.

Logan blinked a few times. "Right! We got a request for a whole evening of silks and music. I thought you and Dani would be a good match, alternating then doing a few things together. They can also do some silks, but they can be the primary musician and you can be the primary aerialist. What do you think?"

"Sure. Send me the details, and we can start to work on a

piece together. What's it for?" Hopefully Dani would be okay with this. It was a lot of time together, and I didn't want them to feel stuck with me or suffocated by my presence.

"It's a fancy corporate anniversary party of some sort. I'll send you the inquiry," Logan said as she began typing on her phone.

"Did you know Bex is helping Dani move in tonight?" I checked my watch and decided I should probably head out in the next hour, since Dani said it would be around 8 p.m. when they would arrive at the house.

"Why would I know what Bex is doing?" Aven scrunched her nose up.

"Bitch, come on, we know there is some tension there," Logan said, and the two of us stared pointedly at Aven.

"And nothing has really happened. We're adults, and it was fun and consensual and a one-time thing. It's not like a serious thing. Plus, I'm not dating right now, and that is that." Aven crossed her arms and scowled.

"And remind me why you're taking a hiatus?" Tilting my head to the side, I tried to feign innocence. Aven was stubborn and stuck to her word, even if it meant she was getting in her own way.

"Because it's like a full-time fucking job on top of what we already do, and I'm tired of people not having their shit together and then trying to drag me in it," she grumbled. We all knew it was more than that. Aven had relationship baggage she didn't like to talk about. She was prickly when it came to her feelings. We often let her come to us when she was ready to talk it out.

"Who said anything about dating? Just continue doing something casual and fun?" Logan shrugged, moving more easily around Aven's rough edges than the rest of us. Logan didn't let shit slide, but Aven got away with more than most.

"No thanks. You aren't dating either, so don't come at me

with this bullshit!" Aven pointed an accusatory finger at Logan, who brought her hand to her chest in a dramatic gesture.

"Because I'm also busy, and casually dating is not my jam. I cannot sleep with anyone without having somewhat of an emotional connection first, so it counts me out of some of the dating fun."

I couldn't even remember the last time anyone had piqued Logan's interest in the least bit. She often chewed men up and spat them out.

"Not that this hasn't been fun, but I will let you two work out your single woes while I head to my house to prepare for Dani." I stood up and offered hands to both of them to haul them to their feet.

"Call if you need backup," Aven added as I gathered my things to head out the door.

"Logan already gave me the talking to about it. I will let you all know. Unless you just want to come because of Bex," I teased. The urge to press her buttons was strong. Bex was a catch, and so was Aven. Why didn't she just let fate take care of the rest?

"Not you too, Myla," Aven whined and pouted.

"Byeee!" Logan waved, pulling Aven into her office to help her with something else.

I texted Dani asking for an update, and they said they were coming over with all their things and Bex's truck in tow. Perfect. The three of us could handle it. From my understanding, it was really just their bedroom furniture since they had moved into an empty room while their brother's friends had furnished the rest of the house.

Pulling up, I tried to make sure the pathway was clear for them to get their stuff in and that there wasn't anything hanging out in the extra room. It had been Jake's storage space, but everything had gotten shoved out when his butt had been shoved to the curb. It was empty now, just waiting for someone to come inhabit it.

Gently, I tried to walk back into my room and make amends with my bed. I still felt deeply uncomfortable sleeping there. Maybe the couch would be my home for a while. Panic racked my body. Crap. How would I explain that to Dani? Wouldn't that be kind of weird? I hadn't come up with a real plan for that yet.

The doorbell rang, interrupting my spiral, and I hustled over to where Dani and Bex stood smiling, holding boxes and suitcases. I would need to think of a story later, because it was too late now.

"You're here!" I squealed and ushered them in.

"Hi, Myla. Pleasure to see you again," Bex said, his accented voice warm and low.

"You too, thanks for helping," I said, looking at a slightly mussed-up Dani.

"It shouldn't take too many trips. Hopefully we can get it done fast," they said, and we got to work. Dani was right. There wasn't a ton of stuff. We got all the boxes in just a few short trips.

"It's really just the bed and mattress that will be annoying," Dani commented as we all worked together to unload the furniture and move it into the room. Dani went to work assembling the bed frame as we moved the rest of the furniture in. We worked like a well-oiled machine getting things in, unpacked, and put together. Overall, the process only took a couple hours.

"Do you want to stay for food or something? I feel like I should feed everybody," I said as we all sat around slightly sweaty and exhausted.

"Sure, I could eat." Bex grinned. His eyes sparkled like he was always up to mischief. I was sure he could go toe to toe with Aven, but she would let us into her business when she was ready.

"Great! How about some Indian food?" I pulled up the menu, and we all decided on our orders. I called it in and offered to go pick it up as Bex and Dani attempted to continue organizing Dani's things.

When I came back, they had made it through a decent amount of all the piles. The closet looked more full, as did their bathroom. It felt nice to have someone besides Jake filling the space. It made the house feel less empty. Like it was less broken.

"Geez you all are fast!" I laid out the food on the counter.

"I didn't have much stuff really." Dani shrugged, and we all ate in relatively comfortable silence before Bex said his goodbyes and headed out.

"So, our first night as roomies," I said, looking at Dani, who smiled in return.

"Yes! Are there any rules or things I should know?" Dani asked.

"Um, I really haven't gotten that far. Maybe don't be an asshole?" I shrugged.

Dani chuckled, and the sound was beautiful music to my ears. "Got it, maybe we'll talk more about it tomorrow. I think I'm going to shower and then head to bed. Training and moving has me exhausted. Maybe we can do a little house run-through and rule set-up tomorrow?"

"Sounds great." I cleared our plates and exhaled a sigh of relief. I wouldn't have to explain why I was sleeping on the couch tonight. Maybe I could avoid it for a while if Dani normally turned in early.

This would be great. Maybe the couch would be less horrible tonight now that there was another human being here who wasn't an annoying asshat.

Surely things would be better, right?

TEN
DANI

The sun streamed into my new bedroom window. The room was cozy and well lit. Much nicer and spacious than the room I had been crammed into for the last few months. I was grateful for the temporary housing, but this felt like a home. Like I could finally take a full inhale and exhale comfortably.

Plus, I had a personal bathroom, and I just felt like I could take up space here with Myla, like she was just as excited as I was to live together. I couldn't have asked for a better solution for my lessons either. Not to mention I could practice during the day when Myla was out; no need to worry about any noise complaints. It was truly wonderful.

And we might be getting a pet?! What more could I ask for. This was the best-case scenario.

Yawning, I got up and headed to the bathroom to brush my teeth before I saw Myla. We would need to talk about any ground rules she had with cleaning or cooking or anything else that needed to be addressed. Rules were helpful for me, and boundaries were necessary. This was her space first and fore-most, and I wanted to respect that. It could be my space too, but I wanted to be a good friend and a great roommate. I had the utmost faith we could work out a lovely living situation.

Slipping on a pair of fuzzy slippers, I padded into the living room, where Myla was snoring gently on the couch. Her mouth was slightly open, and her purple hair created a halo around her. Right now she looked peaceful, like the intensity of the last few weeks—hell, really the last few months—didn't exist. The picture made my heart squeeze, but I wondered if she had slept out here?

Furrowing my brow and tiptoeing around her, I went to the other door down the hall to where her room was. At least, that's where we had taken a lot of Jake's shit out of, so I was making an educated guess since there weren't a lot of other options.

The bed looked exactly the same as it had when we'd moved everything out the other day. No pillows or comforter askew, just a pristine picture. Was she having trouble sleeping in her own bed? Was there something wrong with it, or maybe it held some bad memories?

Sneaking back into the living room, I tried to gently roam through her pantry and her fridge. Some eggs, toast, and coffee seemed like a nice way to wake someone up. I got to work, being careful not to make too much noise. Why would she be sleeping on the couch? I couldn't think of anything I had done, but rather, I wondered if the bed signified something else for her.

Hopefully the smell of breakfast would wake her and not me fumbling around trying to find utensils and pans to make breakfast. It was quick work to get it all together, and suddenly Myla groaned. Anticipation spiked in my belly as she rose.

"Dani?" She popped her head up from the couch. A little drool was on her chin, and her hair clung to one side of her face.

"Good morning, Myla." I walked over to the dining room table and set some plates down, making a few trips to grab the food and coffee. Wow, she looked cute all disheveled. I tried to tamp down that thought and focus on the food in my hands. This was not the time to think of how adorable she looked first thing in the morning. It was the exact opposite of what a platonic roommate would do, and I needed to get that under control.

"Did you make breakfast?" Her voice was still sleepy as she blinked her eyes to adjust to the morning light.

"I did. Not sure how you like your eggs, but I thought scrambled was a safe bet," I said.

"Scrambled is a good choice. You didn't have to do that." She stretched her arms, and then a look of alarm flashed across her features, like she suddenly realized I had found her on the couch.

"Um... I fell asleep on the couch I guess," she mumbled, and I raised one of my eyebrows. Myla was a bad liar—something to tuck away for another time.

"Myla, how do you take your coffee?" I poured a cup and set it in front of the plate opposite of me and waved her over.

"A dash of sugar and a splash of oat milk." She avoided my gaze as she shuffled over in a pair of boxer shorts and a long shirt. A pink hue rose on her cheeks, and she cleared her throat as she plopped down.

I took another trip to the fridge and fidgeted around in the cabinet until I found what I was looking for.

"This is really nice. You didn't have to do this at all." Myla licked her lips before she ate her first forkful of eggs. "These are great," she said around the food.

"Thank you, but you provided the food. I should be thanking you. Sorry I rifled through your cabinets and fridge for all the ingredients." A prickly feeling ran along my spine. Maybe this wasn't the best way to go about starting our new roomie relationship. Did I overstep? Maybe Myla hated break-fast foods?

"Please don't apologize. You can make me breakfast anytime." Myla dove into her coffee and sighed. That brought a smile to my face, and my shoulders relaxed slightly.

"Myla, did you really fall asleep on the couch?" I eyed her over my steaming cup. I didn't want to put her on the spot, but I was worried Myla would keep it all to herself if someone didn't ask.

She swallowed audibly and avoided my gaze. "Uh..."

"Myla?" I prodded.

"I tried to get rid of my old mattress because I just couldn't sleep in there, but it fell through. Then I tried a dumb air mattress, and it deflated after an hour of sleep, so... Right now the couch is my bed," she said, pushing her break-fast around her plate.

"Is the bed giving off weird vibes since Jake left?" It was my guess as to what was going on. "You don't have to tell me, but you can talk to me, if you want."

"It does. And, god, it doesn't make any sense because Jake stayed on the couch for the last few months, but it doesn't hold the same memories. I can't even remember the last time we slept together, but every time I lie down, I'm flooded by the memories of what happened." She buried her face in her hands. Her eyes had gone watery, and small sniffles escaped from her.

"I get that."

"And truly the couch isn't that bad, you know? I can stay on it for a while. It's better than the blow-up mattress riddled with holes." Myla snatched a piece of toast and slathered it with butter.

"I have a different idea." The thought was kind of wild, but it would be temporary, and Myla deserved better than this.

"What's that? You aren't allowed to buy me a mattress, so that better not be it." She pointed her fork at me aggressively.

Giggling, I rolled my eyes. "Put the fork down, Myla. No, I'm not going to buy you a mattress."

"A sleeper sofa?" she hypothesized.

"Stop your guessing and just let me tell you."

"Okay, what is it?" Myla grinned at me, tilting her head.

"Share my bed with me," I stated. Maybe it was an odd idea, but my bed was more than big enough for two of us to share, at least for a short while. Maybe it would help desensitize me to Myla's presence and make the crush go away. This was her house, and she shouldn't have to avoid sleeping in a bed because of her dumb ex-boyfriend.

"That wouldn't be weird for you?" Myla's eyes widened.

"I don't think so. It would be like a never-ending sleepover for a bit. Would it be weird for you?" I countered. People had sleepovers with friends all the time where they shared the same bed. Myla was an athlete, and sleeping on the couch or floor could be detrimental to her physical and mental health.

"I don't think so. Do you snore?" she asked.

"Not as badly as you do," I teased. Her mouth dropped open.

"Oh my god, was I snoring?!" She groaned and threw her head back.

"It was more like light snuffling." I did an imitation of the little snorts and sounds she'd made. She busted out laughing, and it made my stomach do a little flip.

"Okay, well, if you can deal with my snuffling, then I think we have a deal." She held out her hand to shake on it.

"What are we shaking on exactly, Myla?" I curled one eyebrow up and fought the urge to tug on my ear.

"That we will sleep together until I figure this out." She wiggled her fingers at me.

"Fine, we have a deal." And we shook on it.

"You aren't, like, a cover hog or an aggressive snuggler, are you?" Myla asked, tapping her chin.

"I mean, it's too late now. We practically signed it in blood." This banter definitely wasn't flirting, but just two friends having a good time. At least that's what I kept telling myself, because I had just asked Myla to share my bed with me in a platonic way. No tomfoolery here.

She rolled her eyes and finished off her breakfast. "Thank you again for the food, and for sharing your bed. I know this is kind of... funny."

"Don't sweat it. I'm happy to share my bed with you, considering you're sharing your house with me." I meant it too. It felt like the least I could do.

"I still think we should get a pet," Myla said happily.

"Agreed. We should set a time to go look at the local shelters. Maybe sometime next week?" I asked.

"It's a date!" Myla clapped excitedly, and I tried to hide my blush. She obviously didn't mean it like that. It was just a thing people said, right? "Let me clear the dishes since you did all the work."

I got up and went to get ready for my day. But Myla grabbed my arm, and it sent tingles across my skin.

"Thank you, Dani. You have made this morning much more bearable," she whispered. I fought the urge to wrap her up in my arms and give her a big squeeze.

"Of course. Let me know if you think of anything else for house rules, like cooking and cleaning."

"Yeah, yeah, I'll think about it later." She waved me off as she cleaned off the table.

I headed to the bathroom to get ready and took a deep breath. Was I imagining vibes between Myla and me? Or was it just me that felt the attraction?

I tried not to dwell on it too much as I got organized for my day. My private music clients were all scheduled for later, so I took some extra time setting up my instruments. Methodically, I set out my violin, flute, clarinet, and viola.

They were my prized possessions. I hardly let anyone near them or touch them, because they were worth a lot to me emotionally and financially. Grabbing my portable music stands, I set everything up with chairs in the living room.

"It looks good." Myla beamed at me from the hallway, and I nearly jumped.

"I didn't know you were still here. Is this okay? I'll put everything back once I am done, of course." I wrapped my arms around myself.

"I'm leaving in a few. But you're totally fine. Just use the space however you need."

"Also, if you're okay with it, I'll set up a shared calendar with you showing when I have students coming over so it's not a surprise."

"That is very considerate of you, Dani." Myla continued to beam at me.

"Of course. If there's anything else you need, let me know. Like an aggressive pair of noise-canceling headphones or better insulated walls, you name it," I said, trying to lighten the mood.

Myla giggled and gathered her things. "I'll let you know. I left a house key and a garage door opener for you. And I'll see you later?"

"Thank you! Yeah, I'll see you later," I replied.

Waving, she walked out the door. My heart was beating a million miles a minute, and I couldn't help the stupid grin that spread across my space.

Tonight, Myla would sleep in my bed. And I really couldn't think of any other way I would like to end my day.

ELEVEN
MYLA

I hadn't told anyone where I was going. I probably should have. That would have been the responsible thing to do. I texted Dani saying I was on a date at the coffee shop a few miles from the house and to not stress about it unless they didn't hear from me within a couple of hours. Then maybe call the police. For good measure, I took a screenshot of the guy's profile and sent it to them.

Ugh, the patriarchy sucked.

"Myla!" a deep voice said, and I looked up to see my date.

"Mark, hi, how are you?" I asked.

He went straight in for a hug, and I awkwardly wrapped my arms around him. He was attractive in a traditional sense. He was broad, white, and had light-brown hair with dark-brown eyes. Almost like I had made a Ken doll for myself.

His profile said he was in finance and liked to hang out with his dog and go hiking. There had been no immediate red flags, which I took as a good sign even though there wasn't anything particularly unique or interesting about him otherwise.

"I'm better now that I'm here with you." The charm just

oozed off him. Oddly, it was kind of off-putting. Maybe that was just a *me* problem from being rusty on dating.

My phone buzzed, and I fought the urge to look at it as I was sure it was Dani confirming they had gotten my messages loud and clear. I knew I could trust Dani to keep it between us. If I told Logan or Aven, they would tell everyone else, as well as Jess. And if Jess knew, then so would Ozzie, and then literally everyone at the studio would be gossiping about it.

"How are you, Myla?" Mark asked.

I blinked, not realizing I had spaced out for a second there. Wow, I was already doing a bad job here. This would be fun, right? I just had to relax and enjoy this moment.

"I'm good. Sorry, I had an intense day of training. Uh, do you want to get something to drink?"

This part of dating was horribly awkward. Did you wait for your date to get there to order something? Was it weird to order something before? And what about the pay situation? All these silly rules were remarkably dumb.

"Yeah, my treat. What can I get you?" He made it easy, and for that I was grateful.

My shoulders relaxed a little. "I'll take a medium cold brew with a splash of oat milk."

"Oh, you're one of *those* people?" he teased, and I scrunched up my nose.

"What?" That felt oddly confrontational.

"You don't believe in dairy?" he asked, tone serious. My mouth dropped open in a little *o* before I could compose myself.

"I just like oat milk." I furrowed my brows at him. What a weird thing to say. Why would I need to justify my milk choice to someone I'd just met? What if I had a dairy allergy or something?

"I'm just teasing." He flashed his perfect smile at me, and I tried to refrain from wincing. Maybe he was just nervous and needed some time to chill out. He ordered a hot chocolate and honestly, if he was going to be judgy about my drink, I had some judgments for his.

"So you're in finance?" I started, wanting this weird small talk to get less terrible.

"Yeah, I love it. It's just obscenely competitive and such great money." He sipped his drink with easy confidence.

"That does sound... fun." It sounded absolutely horrible. But I couldn't exactly tell him that.

"I'm sure you're also super competitive as a circus performer." He stated it like it was a fact, and I titled my head to the side. That felt like another odd thing to say. Maybe I was just reading into things, or maybe he just was kind of a jerk.

"I'm not sure I know what you mean."

"Like you're always trying to beat out other people to be better and stronger, you know?" Mark seemed very confident about his answer. I blinked a few times, trying to figure out how to articulate my words in a way that wouldn't be too aggressive.

"Actually, that's not what circus is about at all. It's about artistry and community. There is really no right way to do anything. There are more safe and unsafe ways. It's not really about being better than anyone but yourself. No one is the best at art or creativity. You just create and play." My voice grew louder with each word. The passion in me was starting to build to almost a wave of anger and irritation. I took a few calming breaths so as not to go off on this guy within the first five minutes. *Why would he presume to know anything about what I do?*

"Oh, that's kind of dumb." He looked disappointed. My eye twitched a little, and something in me cracked. Clearing my throat, I took another deep breath. I was over this date already.

"You know what? I actually have somewhere else—" I didn't get to finish my sentence, because a young, blonde woman stomped up to our table and slammed her hands down.

"Mark, are you fucking kidding me?" she screamed in his face, and my mouth dropped open.

"Stacey, what are you doing here?" Mark nearly fell out of his seat.

"I don't know who you are." She whirled on me, and I instantly stood up and took a step back.

"This is literally a first date, and I was just leaving." I didn't want any part of what was about to go down.

"Don't go on any more because Mark is a piece of shit and a cheating bastard!" she yelled.

"Stacey, why would you say that?" Mark was now standing, trying to usher her away.

"You know what, I don't need to be a part of this. I'll be going and never talking to you, like, ever again." Awkwardly, I saluted them and scurried off, listening to the sounds of their bickering as I ran to my car.

"Son of a bitch," I murmured. Whatever that was, I needed to get the hell away from it. It took me less than ten minutes to get to my house, and Dani's car was there. Would I have a story for them. Had that really just happened? Was my life just a series of unfortunate dating events at this time?

As soon as I walked in the door about to yell for story time, I stopped in my tracks. There was a beautiful violin playing. It was soulful and yearning. The waves of music and swells of sounds made my heart ache and tears prick my eyes.

Tiptoeing in, I saw Dani at one of their music chairs, eyes closed and swaying side to side as they stroked the cords of the violin. I swallowed, trying not to imagine what other types of things those elegant hands could do. They looked magnificent.

I hadn't heard such beautiful and heartfelt music in what felt like years.

My feet were cemented to the floor as my soul was transfixed by the love and heart in each note. Finally, the song came to an end, and Dani opened their eyes.

"Oh my god!" they yelped, momentarily looking absolutely terrified.

"I'm sorry. I didn't mean to scare you or just stare at you like a complete weirdo. You just cast the most beautiful soundspell with your music, and I was utterly bewitched." I made my way to plop down on the couch. What a lovely thing to come home to after an absolutely horrendous date.

"Oh, it's totally fine. I didn't realize you were here, otherwise I wouldn't have played that loudly." They blushed. I hadn't meant to intrude. They were intensely open and honest when they played. I hoped I hadn't made them uncomfortable. Heat rushed to my cheeks.

"Please play more. This house feels aggressive when it's quiet. Too much room for my anxiety to expand. Music makes it feel more full." At least with music, I could let it wash over me and feel something besides this weird emptiness in my chest.

"I get it. Music helps settle my body in ways other things just can't even touch." They slowly put their violin in its case, then tugged on their ear. I felt like I'd totally ruined the moment and their practice session.

"Want to hear a horrible story?" Maybe changing the subject here would be better.

"Uh... sure?" Dani gave me a funny look.

"My date was *truly* tragic. He was annoying from the start. Very typical straight white guy, and then an ex-girlfriend showed up."

"Stop it!" Dani giggled. The tension in the air seemed to fizzle out.

"I'm serious. She said he was a cheating bastard. Which there's just a lot to unpack there. We don't need to scream at someone in a coffee shop, you know? Even if he is a lying prick. Maybe don't feel the need to add a random bystander into your drama." I threw an arm over my eyes and exhaled loudly.

"That was nothing like I expected." Dani's continued giggles made the hole in my chest feel less expansive.

"Same honestly." I laughed too at the ridiculousness of it.

"I'm surprised you're dating, Myla. I mean, this all just happened. No judgment, just an observation." Dani came to sit on the chair next to me. On paper, it did all seem to be happening very fast, but my relationship had been over for a long time.

"Jake and I were done long before we actually broke up. It feels like it was just a ticking time bomb ready to explode. Neither one of us had the courage to end it until one day, I miraculously did. I don't know if this is a good idea or not, but I'm trying it out anyway. Probably won't make it worse, right?" I sat up and looked at them expectantly.

"I mean, I'm no relationship expert, so I think it's up to you. But I also think there's nothing wrong with taking the time to process and heal. You know your body and heart best. For all I know, the cure for a breakup is dating more shitty straight men," Dani replied.

"Alright, alright." I waved them off, smiling. This was realistically *not* the cure, but maybe it would make me feel better? So far, it had done the complete opposite.

"Want to watch a movie or something?" they asked. I nodded, and we settled on a Disney movie. It was my comfort whenever things felt like shit, and Dani didn't seem to mind.

I basically fell asleep ten minutes in. Clearly, the emotions of the day had caught up to me. Before I knew it, Dani's gentle voice and hands were waking me up.

"Myla," they whispered.

I groaned, turning over.

"We both know the couch is a bad option. Do you want to give my bed a try tonight?" they asked in a soothing voice.

This quickly woke me up. The thought of sleeping together felt way more intimate than it had earlier when I'd agreed to it. This shouldn't feel like a weird thing to do, but suddenly my nerves were on high alert.

"Uh, yeah. Let me just get ready for bed, and I'll meet you there." I sat up quickly as Dani turned off the TV and checked the doors.

Would sleeping together be odd? The only one who would make this weird would be me. I could be cool. This was just two people sharing and cohabiting a bed together because I couldn't face my silly fears. What could be weird about that?

TWELVE
DANI

There was something about a bedtime routine that was really hard. Probably my neurodivergence making the small task of brushing my teeth seem like the most egregious thing. But I tried to go through the motions and change into my pajamas—just a pair of athletic shorts and a T-shirt. It didn't help that it was my and Myla's first night sleeping together.

She hadn't come in yet, and I had butterflies. The idea of her sleeping next to me for hours made my skin itch. Which side did she normally sleep on? What if she touched me or tried to talk to me in her sleep? What would I do if either of those things happened?

This was my bed, though, therefore I should sleep on the side I regularly sleep on and she could just go on the other side. That wasn't rude, right? It was fine. I stripped off my mountain of pillows, then climbed into my side and lay there like a vampire in its coffin—rigidly straight with my hands folded across my stomach.

"Uh, hey," Myla squeaked in the doorway, and I shot up aggressively. Taking a breath, I tried to appear at ease.

"Hey, I normally sleep on this side of the bed. Hope that side is okay?" I tried to make it sound like a question, but maybe it came off as a demand. Why was I this nervous?

Myla had piled her hair on top of her head and wore a similar pajama set to what I was wearing. This was fine. It was like a totally innocent sleepover that would go on for a prolonged time. It didn't matter that I thought Myla's skin looked good enough to lick, or that the way she smiled made my heart glow. This was like exposure therapy, and I would soon be rid of this crush and be able to move on with my life.

"This side is fine, of course," she blurted, then scurried over with her phone in hand. "Thank you again for doing this. God, I feel like such a coward not being able to face a freaking bed." Myla lowered herself down and stared up at the ceiling, so I did the same.

"You just ended the relationship. It's okay to have conflicting and intense feelings, Myla." The urge to reach out and grab her hand was strong. I really wanted to comfort her, but I knew that would be beyond weird. An image of us spooning together flashed into my mind, but I mentally batted it away. This was not the time or place to think about our bodies pressed up against one another.

"I know. It's just all awfully messy in my head. And why did I go on that terrible date today?" She turned and buried her head in the pillow, and the sight of it made me giggle.

"You're adorable when you're having a tantrum." I turned to face her, and she wiggled into her pillow some more. The date really had been an absolute disaster.

"I'm glad this is attractive." She kicked her legs dramatically. The sight of it did funny things to my core. I tried to ignore the feelings rustling underneath my skin.

Myla is my friend and roommate. My friend and roommate. Friend and roommate.

Clearing my throat, I turned to look back up at the ceiling.

"He's a dumbass for not seeing you as the wonderful human being and performer you are. You deserve someone who sees you for you and supports the things you love, including oat milk."

Silence seemed to fill the room, and I was afraid I had said something wrong. That I had put my foot in my mouth, and I wanted to groan. My goal wasn't to make Myla feel worse. Sometimes things just spilled out without much thought.

"Thank you, Dani. That's very sweet of you to say," Myla whispered from beside me, and I peeked over to where she was now lying on her back.

"Goodnight." I clicked off my lamp, and darkness fell over us.

"Goodnight," she muttered.

I turned away and tried not to be hyperaware of her presence. Soon her breathing evened out, and I knew she must have fallen asleep. I felt like every hair on my body could feel her body next to me. How the hell was I supposed to sleep? I already had trouble with insomnia.

I popped a few melatonin and tried to count backward from one hundred. Eventually I drifted off, but not without thoughts of Myla's body doing very different things in this bed with me, all of which blew away past friends and roommates.

———

My eyes flew open to see Myla's face inches from mine. Her plump lips opened slightly, and her hair was a halo of purple around her. She was extremely close to me. My breath caught in my throat as I tried to map the outline of her skin permanently in my head. She was so extraordinarily beautiful, it hurt. My fingers itched to reach out and stroke her cheek.

Not wanting her to wake up and think I had lost my mind, I slowly tried to slink out of bed and go to the bathroom. She looked positively ethereal in my bed. The urge to take a picture was strong, but I would absolutely not be doing that. At all. Ever.

As I got ready, I tried not to think of the way Myla's shorts had risen over her ass or that her shirt had lifted to show the skin of her belly.

Swallowing, I tried to force myself to focus on the task at hand, which was showering quickly and quietly. She slept through the whole thing, and I made it to the kitchen to make breakfast again. There. That wasn't so bad. This would get less awkward, and I would get less horny, surely.

Today, I made pancakes with a smoothie on the side. And always coffee.

"Dani, what in the world smells that heavenly?" Myla floated out of my room, looking rumpled and sleepy.

"I made some pancakes and some smoothies. Want some?" I gestured for her to sit down, and she plopped down at the table.

"Wow, is this the kind of roomie you are? You're spoiling me here. And you don't have to share or make food for me," she mused as I set the table in front of her. I liked feeding her, though—taking care of her. A small part of me was purring from watching her eat my food and sleep in my bed. How weird was that? What was I, a caveman?

I had no right to feel that way, but I did. I would just keep those thoughts to myself.

"What would you be having if I weren't here?" I raised a brow at her.

"Maybe like a granola bar?" Myla answered.

"How about we split groceries and I can commit to doing some of the cooking, and you can do the cleaning?" That seemed like more than fair trade for the both of us. Plus, she needed to be eating more with her training schedule. A granola bar would not cut it for the intensity in which she moved regularly.

"Deal." Myla dove right into the pancakes, groaning with each bite, which had me blushing a bit.

"Cooking is sort of a love language, you know? Something about feeding people makes me feel good and is a way to show I care about someone." I spoke the words into my pancakes and was afraid to look up to where Myla was beaming at me.

"I'm honored to be eating your food then. I made your bed, which is my way of showing you I also care." Myla tilted her head at me, looking sheepish. Another image of her folded over my bed and reaching for the covers with her ass cheeks out popped into my head, and I took a gulp of scalding coffee to try and chase it away.

"Wow, that was really nice. Thank you, Myla." My chest warmed at the thought of her straightening out the sheets and taking the time to impress me.

"We make a good team, don't you think?" Myla asked, and I nodded.

"The best." I would be on her team any day of the week if she asked me to.

"I'm going to head to the studio soon to train before I come back and deal with some of my private music clients. Are you okay with cleaning this up?" I waved around at the scattering of plates.

"For sure. I'll see you later!" Myla pulled out her phone, and I took that as my cue to leave.

Bex and I had agreed to meet at the studio today for a morning session, and I didn't want to be late. It took me less than twenty minutes to get there, where he was already warming up his handstands. My body was buzzing with trapped energy, partly because I couldn't stop my thoughts from lingering on Myla and the way I wanted to wrap her up and never let her go.

"Hey! Are you getting in the air at all today?" I asked as I began my warm-up.

"Maybe. I might do some sling today, but I want to puzzle out some of my hand-balancing act. How are the first few nights of your living situation going?" He raised one of his eyebrows at me. It had a notch out of it that made him seem edgy and infinitely cool.

"It's good," I said curtly. I didn't want to reveal any of my feelings, and Bex seemed keen to meddle. He had peppered me with questions the other day, and I swear to god he knew my crush on Myla was growing faster by the minute. Maybe if I kept everything locked down, he wouldn't be able to sniff out my wild pheromones.

"That's all?" Bex narrowed his eyes at me.

"Yeah, that's all." Was I that transparent? I needed to bury it before I freaked Myla out. The last thing I wanted was for her to be uncomfortable.

"Hmmm..." He eyed me suspiciously.

"Do you have something to say, Bex?" I quipped.

"Just that it appears there might be something else going on between the two of you, but what do I know. Maybe you have a little crush?" he teased as he did a few kick ups. I was going to kill him. But first, I needed a way not to wear my heart on my sleeve.

"Bex! There is nothing going on. And even if I did have a crush on Myla, she just got out of a relationship, and we are roommates. Her emotional state is fragile, and she doesn't have a ton of experience dating other queer people. And none of this matters anyway, because Myla and I are just friends. And having a crush on her would be highly inappropriate!" I tumbled over my words and threw him a look. Maybe if I said all those words enough times, they would actually be true.

"Methinks you doth protest too much," he purred in his stupidly confident English accent.

"Whatever. Nothing is happening between us, and you should mind your business," I scolded him. He shrugged like my tone didn't bother him in the least bit.

"You know I can't do that. Also, everyone is going to a drag show I have coming up in a few weeks. You and Myla in?" Bex's eyes danced mischievously.

"I don't know about her, but I'm in."

"I mean, you could relay the information since you live together." He had that dumb look on his face again, like this whole thing amused him greatly.

"Sure," I grumbled.

"Oh, Dani... You're in trouble for sure," Bex teased as he sauntered off to the warehouse.

Just because my heart felt warm and fuzzy when Myla was around didn't mean I liked her that much. And just because I thought she was beautiful and wonderful didn't mean I had the urge to date her.

I had more control than that. Didn't I?

I guess we would find out.

Thirteen

Myla

I'd made another horrible mistake. This was going to be my fourth tragic date with a man I had met online dating. Was it a self-fulfilling prophecy if I began the date with this attitude? Maybe. But realistically, I could feel it in my gut that this was going to be bad.

Obviously date number one with Mark was terrible, because what could really be salvaged from a date where your ex-girlfriend rudely jumped in and insulted you in front of your current first date? Not to mention his weird attitude about my job and the oat milk. Lots of red flags for that one.

So that one had gone downhill from the beginning.

Then there was Josh. He had been thirty minutes late and had said he thought we were meeting later, even though he was the one who'd set the time. I should have left, but I'd ended up reading a book on my phone and being so engaged with it that I'd forgotten all about time and space around me. Josh had shown up right as the spice was about to happen. Typical. He had been about as interesting and enthralling as a blank, white wall. I should have asked him to leave so I could spend quality time with the novel and book boyfriend in hand.

The last one had probably been the worst. Paul had kept commenting on how attractive I was and how he couldn't believe I was real. What the actual heck was that supposed to mean? What really broke the date was the fact his contact had popped out at one point, and he first put it in his glass of water to try and save it and then fished it out to put it back in his eye. I had watched in horror as this all took place, wondering why I was bearing witness to such an odd event on a first date.

When that hadn't worked, he put it in his mouth. His actual *mouth*. That felt like something that happened when you were together for years, not within the first hour of meeting someone. Something about his saliva touching his eyeball really sent me over the edge.

Respectfully, I got up and left. I was under the impression first dates were about putting your best foot forward, but maybe I had been out of the game too long, you know? Or maybe the problem wasn't me, but just men in general. I wanted this to be fun and exciting, not dreadful and exhausting. It was as if every man in my vicinity decided the way to a woman's heart was to be their actual worst, disgusting selves immediately to see if you had the gall to get out quick.

My dating spirit was officially exhausted and, mentally, I was in desperate need of a nap.

"Myla, hi!" Carter walked over to me, and I tried to rally some enthusiasm.

"Hi, Carter. Nice to meet you."

He sat down and was a pretty standard attractive man. I clearly had a type—sort-of-typical, boring, straight-laced guys. My luck with other queer people on the apps was basically non-existent. I wasn't sure if that was a me or them problem. Or an app problem. Maybe all the above?

Things were honestly going fine with Carter, until he brought up he thought women were doing too much these days and that staying home caring for babies was really what they needed to be doing.

Blinking, I stared at him, not sure if I'd registered what he had said.

"Goodbye, Carter." I stood up and strode out, rolling my eyes as he sputtered behind me. I really needed to vet these dates better. Why was I entertaining these crappy experiences? It had been a few weeks since Jake had moved out. He'd tried calling and texting a few times, but I blew him off. What if I just wore a sign around my neck that said "no men, check back in a few months"?

Why couldn't they be kind, caring, and interesting? Someone like Dani. A small smile spread on my lips thinking about how easy things were with them.

Dani and I had fallen into a nice rhythm of domestic roomie bliss. We slept soundly in the same bed, which should have been kind of weird but was oddly nice. They got up and made breakfast, while I made the bed and did the dishes. It was way more pleasant than anything Jake and I had been doing. It felt equitable. Like a true partnership.

I would come home to the sounds of their sweet music playing, filling the house with all types of emotions that felt like I was in my own period-piece drama. It was lovely and made the screaming emotions in my head feel less loud. They were quickly becoming one of my favorite people, and the world didn't feel as lonely with them in it. I just hoped they were enjoying the house as much as I enjoyed having them there. Everything seemed okay, but I fussed over it nonetheless.

However, it did feel really lonely when I went on these stupid dates. I really needed to stop doing that. I was hurting no one but myself. This had been a lunch date because I had to go to the studio later, so I just headed straight there. At least it hadn't lasted that long and I knew quickly it wasn't for me. Better late than never, I supposed.

Pulling up, I noticed almost everyone's cars were there besides Dani's. They had some private music students today, so I was sure I wouldn't see them until I got home. My ears were thankful to be away from the new students Dani trained, but I was a little sad not to see them during the day as much.

"Hi," I shouted as I stepped in and saw the whole crew there. "Ozzie! You're back in the studio!" I ran up to her and gave her a tentative hug, trying to avoid her injured shoulder. Her short, blonde hair was a little rumpled, but otherwise she looked as strong and confident as she always did.

"Yes, I'm approved to do some stretching and some strength stuff. I was losing my mind being at home." Ozzie looked good despite her being gone for a while to heal from her dislocation.

"I could have kept you busy." Jess walked out of the bathroom and winked. Giggling, I looked between the two of them.

"Does that mean you two made up, officially?" I raised an eyebrow. We all knew they had made up; this was just their first public appearance together. It made my heart happy to see them back to their old dynamics. They'd had a romantic rough patch, but eventually they'd worked it all out. Ozzie and Jess were a great couple, it just took the two of them some time to figure that out themselves.

"Yes, we made up." Jess placed a chaste kiss on Ozzie's cheek.

"Thank god, we were all getting a little uncomfy to be honest." Aven gave an exasperated sigh as she walked in from the warehouse.

"Truly could not handle another tragic love story," Logan said, peeking her head out from the office.

"Okay, no need to add the dramatics," Jess grumbled, and Ozzie laughed.

"Anyway, we're all still on to go to Bex's show tomorrow night, right?" I dropped my things on the ground and started moving deeper into the space to warm up.

"Hell yes! Wouldn't miss it," Ozzie said excitedly.

"Yes, we're all excited to see Bex." Logan looked pointedly at Aven, who avoided her eyes. One of these days, Aven would admit to herself that Bex was more important than just someone she hooked up with once. Today was obviously not that day.

"Great. Dani is coming too. Is Bex here, or is he somewhere else today?" I asked, looking around to see if he was hiding out somewhere.

"I think he's prepping for tomorrow since the venue is a bit new to him," Logan answered. We all went off to do our own thing to get ready for whatever we were training today.

"Got it. I'm going to work on my silks piece and then get out of here, because Dani and I are trying this new restaurant tonight!" I was giddy to try this new place Dani had found. It looked really good; I had been bugging Jake to try it before we'd broken up, but he never took any freaking initiative. Dani told me they'd made a reservation basically the day after we had talked about it and asked if I wanted to go. Things could really just be that simple, but Jake always did the least amount of work possible.

"So things are going well between the two of you?" Jess asked casually. Her eyes widened in an innocent stare. Too innocent.

"Really great. It's nice to have them there. We have a good roomie rhythm." Smiling, I thought of how much we seemed to laugh in the evenings just talking about our days. When was the last time I had laughed that much with someone outside of my little circus crew? Certainly not with Jake.

"That's great, Myla." Logan gave me a quick hug, which was sort of weird.

"Okay, don't know why you all are being touchy about this, but yeah, it's good."

"We were just worried after everything with Jake. We love you and just want you to be okay and happy," Aven said gently. They all looked at me like I might break into a million little pieces. I shifted from side to side, a bit uncomfortable underneath all their stares.

"I know. But I'm okay. I've been going on some really terrible dates, but as a whole, I feel a lot better about where things are at." Which was true. Things were looking up. Not necessarily relationship-wise with these men, but my life as a whole felt better.

"Tell me more about these dates!" Ozzie looked like a kid at a candy store.

So for the next few hours, we swapped our terrible dating stories, and it felt good to be with all my friends like this again. Like the world felt a little lighter and brighter today.

————

Walking into my home, I was greeted by the sweet sounds of Dani's flute. I danced in, twirling and swirling with my eyes heavy like I was waltzing through my movie moment. Dani's eyes twinkled, and they stood up, walking around me while playing their sweet melody.

My hands rose as I swayed side to side, and they finished their song.

"Did you like that one?" they asked, smiling.

"I loved it."

"I wrote it, actually." They blushed slightly, and it was the cutest thing I had seen all day.

"Dani, you're majorly talented. It was truly lovely."

They carefully set their flute down in its case. "How was training?"

"Good. I'm pooped, though, and ready to go try this new place." I needed food desperately after the training I'd done today.

"How was your date?" Dani asked, their face unreadable.

"Terrible actually. Like another tragedy," I grumbled.

"Myla, why do you keep going on dates with these terrible men?" Dani laughed, and it was meant to be gentle teasing, but they had a point. I often asked myself the same thing.

"I really don't know. Is my good-partner meter off or something? Because I'm over it already," I said. They really did seem to be getting worse and worse.

"I mean, you haven't dated very much outside of men before, right? Even though you identify as queer?" they asked softly, like the question might scare me away. It was a valid question.

"No. I mean, I realized I was queer while dating Jake, but this is what I know best. It's safe and comfortable, but, like, not actually that comfortable because men are the worst, you know?" I chewed on my lip.

"Maybe you just need some practice at getting comfortable in your own queer identity to get more comfortable dating in that identity?" Dani offered. They seemed super confident in their own gender and sexual identity. I wanted to get to that level of authenticity for myself. It was hard, though, when I had been downplaying who I was for the sake of a relationship that was already failing.

"I think you're right. Society pushes the heteronormative agenda, and it's really hard to push against that. Even with myself, when I know it's not exactly what I want." I knew these things, and yet I kept engaging with it.

"Maybe keep that in mind next time you match with a guy," Dani said softly.

"Thank you, Dani," I said quietly.

"You will probably meet lots of queer people tomorrow at Bex's show. Might be a good opportunity to flex your queer muscles?" Dani teased, and I groaned.

"Ugh, if you insist. But right now, I must eat noodles. Can we go please?" I jumped up and down, ready to consume all the noodly goodness.

"So whiny today," Dani chastised, and I laughed as I grabbed their hand and dragged them to my car.

"Off on a Myla and Dani adventure!" I whooped and hollered, my heart full and my head a little lighter.

Fourteen

Dani

The club was bumping. Disco balls reflected lights that bounced off all the glitter everyone seemed to be donning. Everything was splashed with rainbow, bright colors dripping on every wall and bar in this place. Bex's drag show had been the talk of the town, and it showed.

"This is amazing," I said as our group moved to find our reserved table. The music could be felt in your chest as the beat thumped and bodies swayed side to side.

"Isn't it spectacular?" Aven gushed, looking around at the colorful collection of queer folks congregated for this night of debauchery. Aven seemed to be in especially good spirits tonight. It appeared as though everyone saw that she and Bex could be a great match, except maybe her.

"Woo!" Logan screamed. She had a feather boa she kept tickling people with. Everyone she walked past was absolutely smitten with her, and Logan blew them all a kiss. She was a big flirt but had no intention of following through.

Ozzie and Jess were seated at our table right next to the stage with bright pink cocktails in their hands, heads snuggled in together. They looked absolutely in love with one another, and it made my heart hurt in the best way.

Myla reached for my hand as she dragged me over to the table. Our fingers intertwined naturally as we walked over to greet our friends. Her palm felt warm. I tried not to think too much about it. Friends held hands all the time. It didn't mean anything more than that. I tried to focus on that thought instead of the heat of her palm in mine. I'd hoped our chat the other night about her dating men wasn't too harsh. She was a baby queer in many ways, and I wanted her to be able to explore that. It seemed the men she was picking were a copy-and-paste of her ex. She deserved better than that, and I was doing my best to help her realize that.

"Are you ready?" Myla threw her hands up and shook her hips. God, she looked spectacular. Her hair was in a high ponytail, and she was rocking a tie-dye bodysuit with a white crochet dress over it and white booties.

"Let's get some shots for the table!" Ozzie cheered.

"And drinks!" Aven added.

They all broke off to get us what we needed, as the show was beginning in about ten minutes.

Myla pulled me down to sit next to her. The energy coming off her was positively giddy and wild. She leaned in close to whisper in my ear since the music was quite loud.

"This place is fun. They will release confetti, balloons, bubbles, and all kinds of things throughout the night." She giggled like a kid on their birthday.

"Can't wait," I answered. This wasn't usually my scene, but I was pumped to see Bex and the show. In a few short moments, our friends returned with drinks, and we all took a shot together. I declined my drink, as I usually was a drink or two kind of person a night, sometimes even less. I offered it to Myla, who happily went about double-fisting it with her own.

"Don't worry, I'll ensure everyone makes it home. Have as

much fun as you want," I whispered in Myla's ear, and I swore I saw a little pink tinge on her cheeks. Whispering to each other felt oddly intimate, and it made my lower belly flutter. But it was loud, and otherwise we would be screaming in one another's faces, so this was much better honestly.

The emcee came out and welcomed us all. She was a big and beautiful queen with a full glitter beard and a sparkling evening gown. The whole crowd cheered and hollered as she strutted around and started introducing our queens of the evening.

When it was Bex's turn, we all yelled and hollered our hardest.

"And finally, Bex the Beauty is here, and she is ready to slay!"

"YES, QUEEN!" Aven screamed the loudest out of all of us, and Logan busted out laughing as Bex blew a kiss to her.

Bex the Beauty was in a rhinestone leotard and tall boots. It fit her like a dream, and long, blonde hair ran down her back. Her makeup was flawless. Honestly, Bex was hot. Her tanned skin was dusted over with glitter, and everything about her was sparkly and immaculate.

"Bex is sexy," Ozzie mused, and Jess nodded in agreement.

"I'd tap that for sure," Logan purred.

Aven fanned herself dramatically, and Myla giggled.

The performance consisted of lots of queens dancing, singing, and playing out little skits. Bex, of course, did some hand-balancing that the crowd went wild for, and we all forced a standing ovation when Bex was finished.

Dollar bills were thrown around and tucked into costumes. At one point, Bex came over and gave a very flustered Aven a lap dance, where Logan slid a twenty into Bex's very impressive breasts.

Finally, the show came to an end with hollering from the audience, and the music immediately started up again. The whole crowd was thrumming to the beat. The dance floor seemed to pulse as everyone moved their bodies.

Aven and Bex were grinding heavily on one another. Logan had made her way on top of the bar, and the crowd was eating that shit up. Her feather boa was whipping around as she did jump-splits and rolls. Nobody told her to come down, so she kept moving and grooving.

Jess and Ozzie were making out heavily in the corner, so it was really just Myla and me for ourselves. Something about this night seemed to have lit a fire for everyone to embrace their sexual prowess.

Myla was absolutely drunk, giggling and throwing her hands up and swaying her body. I grabbed her palms and twirled her a few times until she came flying into me, her hands landing around my neck.

"This is soooo fun," she slurred, and I tucked some loose hair behind her ear.

"It is! Bex was incredible."

Myla's cheeks were red, and she licked her lips. Sweat was sliding down between us, but Myla didn't seem to care because all she wanted was to dance and wiggle in the crowd.

"Okay, I'm calling it a night. How is everyone else?" Logan asked, finally making her way over to us off her table.

Aven and Bex had disappeared somewhere, as well as Jess and Ozzie.

"I'm going to guess those four are probably okay. I'll take Myla home. Want me to drop you off?" I asked. Logan seemed okay, but I knew she was a few drinks in.

"Myla, darling, are you ready to go home?" Logan grabbed Myla's face, forcing her to look into her eyes.

"YesI'mready," she said, her words all squished together.

"Great. Let's get the fuck out of here! WOOOO!" Logan hollered until we made it out and I got them both in the car. They both wanted all the music, so we cranked it up and sang the whole way home, dropping Logan off before heading back to our house.

Myla was asleep in the back seat by the time we pulled up, and she looked absolutely delectable with her light snoring filling the space.

"Myla, we're back at the house," I said gently, unbuckling her and shaking her slightly.

"Dani?" she asked sleepily.

"Yes, Myla. Will you get out of the car for me?" I didn't want to jostle her too much, but I needed to get her to bed.

"Okay, if you say so." She death-gripped my hand and hauled herself out, making a beeline for the bedroom.

"Okay wait, slow down!" I laughed, trying to follow her. She whipped her clothes off along the way until she was standing naked in front of our bed.

Oh my god. Oh my god. Oh my god.

"Uh, do you want me to get you some pajamas?" I swallowed, trying not to look at the swell of her breasts or the length of her legs. I desperately wanted to look at her, but she was drunk and this felt wrong.

"No," she said, twirling around so I got a full view of her plump ass and all the muscles in her back.

"Myla, I think you should put clothes on." My words came out choked.

"Dani..." Myla stalked over to me and threw her arms around me.

Oh god, this is how I die.

"Yes?" I whispered as she pressed her nipples against me. What was happening here? I didn't know what to do with my hands. I felt like a horny teenager, way out of my element with her. She was drunk and barely knew what she was doing. I needed to get us both out of this situation.

"I've been thinking about what you said." Her whole body

was flush against mine. She seemed to press into me even harder. My head was spinning as I tried to think and speak straight. My hands hung limply at my sides in an effort to remain chaste.

"What exactly have you been thinking about?" I asked.

"About me not having experience with anyone else but men. And I want to have that experience." Her eyes were full of heat that sent my stomach into butterflies. How long had she been thinking about this? This felt like a dream.

Somebody pinch me please.

"Okay," I whispered, my mouth suddenly going very dry.

"And I think I want to experience that with you," she purred, leaning in closer and walking me back. The bed hit the backs of my knees, and I fell, hitting the soft sheets with Myla on top of me. Her tits were right in my face as she crawled on top of me.

"M-Myla, you're drunk," I stuttered. This was not how I wanted this to happen.

"Not that drunk," she said, and then she dove in with her mouth. Her lips collided with mine, and it was messy and hungry and absolutely scorching. Her tongue tangled with mine, and I gasped as she deepened the kiss and pressed herself against me. Heat licked across my skin as she writhed on top. She nipped and tugged on my lip, groaning against my mouth.

"Myla, no, we can't." I rolled her over so she was lying down, and I got up quickly.

"Please, Dani." She pouted, her bottom lick sticking out, and I wanted to bite it.

"Maybe tomorrow. How does that sound?" I was begging her. I needed her to stop. My body could only take so much, and I didn't want her first experience with me to be some drunken night.

"Fine, but promise to kiss me tomorrow," she mumbled as

she crawled into bed. Still buck-ass naked. I counted to ten silently in my head to calm my racing heart.

"I promise," I said as I helped tuck her in, and she closed her eyes. Her soft snores happened in less than thirty seconds.

Swallowing, I ran and took a cold shower to try and calm my body down. Jesus Christ. Myla was going to be the death of me.

And I think I would happily die at her hands.

FIFTEEN
MYLA

I groaned as Dani ate me out. They were a miracle worker with their tongue. It was like they knew all the places and parts of me to play with. Wow, their mouth felt really good on my pussy, like it belonged there, savoring and sucking my soul right out of my body. This was the best oral sex I had ever had. Why were men so incompetent with their tongues? I didn't know why I would ever let anyone else's mouth on my cunt after this.

"Good girl, Myla. Do you like that?" Dani mumbled against my clit. Jesus Christ, that felt amazing. It took me a moment to find words because I was panting.

"Yes," I gasped as I ground my hips against their lips, pinching my nipples and soaking their tongue. I was close, so close, to coming.

"Don't stop, Dani. Please," I pleaded. I think I would absolutely die if they stopped touching me right now.

"That's right, love. I want you begging for it." Their voice ran over me in a delicious wave that sent my senses on high alert. It caressed my skin and pushed me further into the wave of ecstasy threatening to drown me.

Dani curled their fingers inside me and sucked hard on my

clit, causing me to explode all over them. The orgasm hit me like a freight train. It rippled through my limbs and licked across every fiber of my being. Holy shit. I had never experienced anything like that before. It was never that amazing with Jake.

"Now it's time to wake up, beautiful," Dani said. Their voice was fading away, and I could no longer feel their touch. No, no, no. I didn't want them to leave. And I especially didn't want them to go without me getting a taste of them.

"Dani, where are you going?" I whispered as I looked around, and the room itself began to fade. What was going on? We were just getting started. My mind was buzzing with all the delicious things we could do together. I wanted Dani to come back and fuck me some more, and then I wanted to fuck them.

Slowly things darkened around me, and my eyes felt heavy. I was in a losing fight. No matter what I did, I could no longer move or do anything except simply let the weariness take over. Maybe I would just close them for a minute, then I would wake up and everything would be better. Dani would be back, naked and next to me. Things would be exactly as they were supposed to. We would be together in every single way...

Gasping, my eyes flew open, my dream state shattered. I realized I was back to my reality. Blinking aggressively, I tried to get my bearings. That was a dream? I'd had a sex dream about Dani in the bed we were currently sharing together?! I was the worst human being ever.

Frantically, I looked over to see if Dani was sleeping next to me, and thank god they weren't there. What if they heard something? Or saw something? Or, like, smelled something? I could die of embarrassment.

"Thank Christ," I murmured, and then I looked down at myself and suddenly noticed I was naked?! My tits were just out in the wind. Why was this happening? I never went to bed naked!

The orgasm from my dream still tingled through me.

Gingerly, I reached down and touched my clit. It was still sensitive, swollen, and wet from my dream. Not only did I have a sex dream about Dani, I had a real-life orgasm and I was just sitting in my nakedness. Was there really any way for this to get worse? We were sharing a bed, for goodness' sake. I absolutely could not be doing this.

"I just had a wet dream about Dani." I slapped my hands over my face and groaned. This felt like a surefire way to ruin our arrangement. The thought made me immediately shiver all over. I simply needed to get myself under control, and maybe masturbate a little more. This would be a one-time thing. Never again.

I felt around the bed and realized there was definitely a wet spot. This was the single most embarrassing moment of my life. I would just strip the sheets and wash them, then put them back before Dani even noticed. Working quickly, I grabbed a random pair of Dani's pajamas and slid them over my aching body. What a humiliating way to wake up in the morning.

God, my head hurt like there was a drum line in there. What exactly had happened last night? I was piecing together the memories as I grabbed the sheets and walked out of the room, tiptoeing and trying not to make a big scene, when Dani stepped into the hallway. Freezing mid-step, I was sure I looked like I had just gotten caught doing something bad. They gave me a look I couldn't decipher. This could absolutely not be happening right now.

"Hey," they said softly, and I could barely look them in the eye.

"Hey," I said a bit cheerily, then winced at my loudness, clinging the sheets to my naked chest. "I'm just washing the sheets since, you know, we've been sleeping on them for a minute. And I borrowed your shorts because I was just naked. Which I'm sorry about. I don't know why I threw off all my clothes. And..." Suddenly the rest of the night came crashing into me, taking my breath away.

How I had stripped off my clothes and told Dani I wanted to explore things with them before pinning them down on the bed. The kissing came slamming back into my body, and I took a few steps back. My mouth dropped open.

Oh my god, I had attacked Dani like some sex-crazed monster. Horrified with myself, I swallowed and closed my eyes.

"Myla..." Dani said gently, walking toward me like I was a feral animal.

"Ah!" I squealed, running to the laundry room to dump the sheets. Making quick work of it, I sprinted out and nearly body-slammed Dani, my hands clutching my breasts. Why had I not grabbed a shirt?!

"Myla, it's okay. You don't need to freak out." Dani tried to soothe me, but I felt unhinged.

"Dani, I'm sorry! I attacked you like some horny teenage boy. I can't believe I held you down and kissed you!" I buried my face in my hands, then yelped because now my nipples were out. Why was my brain not working properly anymore?!

"Myla, it's okay."

"No it's not! You didn't ask for that! I just threw myself at you!" I walked into the living room, grabbing a random hoodie I had laying about and turning around to throw it on. I could not have this conversation with my boobs out.

"Myla, take a breath." Dani followed me as my heart seemed to beat a million miles per hour.

"I would totally understand if you didn't want to live here anymore. God, I'm sorry." I sat down and looked at Dani in horror.

"Myla. Can you listen to me for a second?" Dani asked, then sat right next to me.

"Give it to me. Please yell at me if it makes you feel better.

I can take it." I closed my eyes and balled my fists, waiting for Dani's reaction.

Instead, Dani grabbed my hands. "Open your eyes, Myla."

"I'm scared," I said. I was a coward. I had attacked them, yet I was the one acting like a big baby without even considering their feelings. Damnit, I was literally the worst. Their hands felt familiar in mine. Little tingles traveled up my arm, and I tried to ignore the sensation. I didn't deserve to like their touch after everything that had happened in the last twenty-four hours.

"Don't be scared, open your eyes." Dani's breath skittered across my cheeks, and I tried to refrain from squirming in my seat.

I cracked open my eyelids, and they stared back at me. They were extraordinary. Their dark-green eyes reminded me of a lush forest and paired well with their fiery orange hair. It was like they were crafted from the most beautiful parts of nature.

"I'm not mad about last night," Dani said, their voice quiet and low.

"You're not?" I squeaked.

"No. In fact, it wasn't the kissing part I didn't like," Dani said coyly.

"What?" My mind went blank. They didn't hate the kissing part? What was actually happening right now. My eyes flitted to their lips, then back up.

"No, it was that you were drunk and not in your right mind."

"Oh," I mumbled as they leaned in closer, and I looked at their lips again. They were really quite distracting this close.

"But I did promise you something," they said, their lips inches from mine.

"What's that?" I hardly recognized my voice; it was raspy

and needy. My aching center seemed to come alive again, and the urge to touch myself was strong.

"That I would kiss you again." They leaned in and brushed their lips against mine. Heat went straight to my center, and I felt desperate for more contact. Instead, I forced myself to sit there and breathe.

"Dani."

"Yes?" they asked.

"More. I want more," I commanded, and they wrapped their hand around my neck and pulled me in, this kiss unhurried and searing. Our mouths danced with one another as our tongues explored. I moaned as Dani's hand slid down my side, caressing my hips and landing on my ass.

There was a neediness in me that began to build as I made little noises each time Dani's hands explored my skin. I let mine do the same, traveling along the length of their strong arms and shoulders.

Ding.

We jumped apart as a timer went off.

"For the cinnamon rolls." Dani grinned at me goofily.

"Oh my god." I jumped up and touched my mouth gingerly.

"Don't freak out, Myla," Dani warned.

"I'm not freaking out." But my voice was too high and too tight.

"Do you need some time to think about this?" Dani offered, and I nodded, not able to form words. "Okay, I'll leave some breakfast for you and I'll be heading out in a few."

"Okay," I whispered.

"Try not to worry too much in that pretty head of yours," Dani replied, and my stomach dipped. I ran to my bathroom and slammed the door, turning on my shower and grabbing one of my trusty vibrators.

Ugh, I was wound tight.

I went through the image and feeling of Dani touching me once more with their deft hands and their lips gently nibbling on mine. I groaned as I upped the speed and thought of the dream where Dani was stationed right at my clit, licking and sucking, doing their best to get me off.

I ground into my toy.

Thoughts of me exploring Dani's body and playing with them filled my head, and that's what pushed me over the edge, wondering what Dani's sweet orgasms would taste and sound like.

Crying out, I crashed into my pleasure with thoughts of Dani's touch and body filling my head as I rode out my release. But it wasn't enough. I wanted to know what it was actually like; not just a thought in my head, but the real thing.

I turned the shower to ice cold and let it run across my sensitive nipples as I wrapped my arms around my body.

When did I start thinking of Dani this way?

I didn't want to ruin our situation. They were one of my favorite people, and we slept in the same bed for god's sake. This was a terrible idea, right?

There was no way this could go well.

But I guess the only way to find out was to try.

And what was the worst that could happen?

I was really tempted to find out.

Sixteen

Dani

The drag show was a few days ago, and Myla had been avoiding me hardcore ever since. She would come to bed after I had fallen asleep and then be out the door before I had even gotten up. I'm sure it was exhausting to do that, but she was committed to it. It made me grin in a weird way. Myla was tenacious, I would give her that. She needed to come to me in her own time, even though her avoidance was driving me up the wall.

However, today her avoidance had to end, because our rehearsal for the special gig request was today. She would be doing silks, and I would be playing the flute. I totally understood this was a lot to process; however, if she would just talk to me, then I think it wouldn't be as bad as she was building it up to be in her head. Myla seemed to be the queen of over-thinking. Her anxiety brain would turn on, and it was nearly impossible for her to get out of it.

But I wanted to respect her thought process and boundaries. The ball was in her court now, and I was a patient person. My crush on Myla had been building since the day I saw her. My queerness was something I had come to terms with a long time ago, when I'd had immense support from my family and the pressure of dating and finding someone just wasn't there for me. Her journey to finding out who she was and what she wanted was her own, even though my desire for her couldn't be quelled.

My gender identity and sexuality were a part of me I wore proudly. Not that it didn't come with its own hardships, but it wasn't anything I felt I couldn't handle. I hoped she could come to terms with her own identity and start feeling comfortable in it.

I walked into the studio, where Logan, Jess, and Ozzie already were.

"Did anyone see them after?" Logan asked, raising a brow at Jess, who furrowed her dark brows.

"Nah, but they for sure left together. I haven't seen them since that night," Ozzie responded. Her short, spiky blonde hair stuck out in random directions like she'd just woken up.

"What are we talking about?" I asked, coming in and gently setting my stuff down.

"Aven and Bex," Jess said, wiggling her brows.

"Are you gossiping in here?" I tsked at them, only teasing.

"Come on, you can feel the tension between them!" Logan threw her hands up in the air.

"Yeah, you totally can. I think they just need some time to address it," I said. It made me think of my sexual tension with Myla. Could they feel it too? It had been really hard the other day when we had done that nude photo shoot for Ozzie's OnlyFans. My poor body desperately wanted to touch Myla, but I tried to keep my face neutral as she played in the silks with almost all her skin on full display.

Logan gave me a look like she could read my thoughts, and I looked anywhere but her face. Did she have to be that observant?

"I think they left together and had a steamy night. It

wouldn't be the first time. Except Aven is on a dating ban right now. Not sure where Bex falls in line with that, but it doesn't mean she can't fulfill her needs, you know?" Jess said as she walked into the warehouse, and the rest of us followed.

"Speaking of tension..." Logan was way too tuned in to everyone; it made my head spin. We did not need this conversation to go toward me and Myla. Absolutely not.

"Logan, I don't want to hear it," I said loudly, stomping into the warehouse before she could get another nosy question in.

"Hear what?" Ozzie asked innocently, but they all gave knowing looks.

"You know what. You all are a bunch of nosy clowns," I said playfully as I began my warm-up. Logan cackled, and Jess grinned broadly. Ozzie had the nerve to look at me like I didn't even know the half of it.

"Ah, and it looks like someone else has just arrived." Logan waved at whoever walked in, and I could feel in my bones it was Myla. This was not going to be good if all her friends were around, ready to pounce on any morsel of news.

I had no idea where she'd sprinted off to the past few mornings before I had gotten up, but now she didn't have a choice but to face me.

"Hi, Myla!" Jess said enthusiastically.

"Hi, Jess," Myla replied.

"Why didn't you two ride together?" Ozzie was poking the bear at this point.

"Um, I had something to do this morning." Myla tugged at her purple hair and avoided everyone's gaze as she scurried to set up her silks.

"Yes, Myla has been very busy the last few days," I teased, and Logan's mouth opened in a little *o*.

"I can't wait to see what you two come up with here. Do

you want a little audience?" It was phrased as a question, but everyone sat down like the only possible answer was yes. They were not going anywhere anytime soon, so it was best to just let them watch.

"Sure. But let us warm up some. This is mostly improv and ambient, so there won't be much to see. It's just me getting familiar with Dani's song and our timing," Myla mumbled, like she didn't want to be here at all. She would have to look at me at some point, but clearly she was determined to hold out as long as possible.

There wasn't much rehearsing that needed to be done. It was just a good idea to run through a couple of our songs from the setlist and let me try them with different instruments. A run-through of what to expect was normal before gigs like this. It didn't need to be a rigid rehearsal, just a gentle walk-through.

"Great! Take as much time as you need. We will just be right here." Logan sat in a straddle with her chin on her palms like she had nothing better to do.

Snickering, I grabbed my music stand and gathered my flute and viola. In the meantime, Myla warmed up on the silks while pointedly avoiding everyone in the room. After fifteen minutes, I was ready, and so was Myla.

"Okay, let's do this." I sat, and Myla stepped up to the fabric.

Slowly, I played a rendition of "Sweet Dreams" on the violin, and Myla went to work. It was like the whole world around us faded, and there was just me and her. The music poured from me easily. It was a piece I was familiar with, one that was lovely for Myla's musicality.

Myla moved effortlessly and poetically through poses and transitions. She began by dancing on the ground and using the fabric as a prop. She moved and made shapes that captivated me, even as I played. I tried to match the swell of her energy as she would travel to the top of the silk and spiral down. Her sequencing of finding beautiful poses and shapes to hold while mixing in quick and dynamic transitions was smart and artistic in a way that had me bewitched.

One song went into three, and as the pace changed, so did she. Her energy and athleticism seemed unmatched, and it was truly breathtaking to watch. I had tears in my eyes from the way she'd manipulated the fabric and her body.

"Woooo!" Logan clapped. Ozzie and Jess joined in her hollering as Myla took a little bow, and I did the same.

"That was great. You'll both be fine for this part of the gig." Logan looked pleased with both of us.

"Is there another part?" I asked, thinking it was only going to be me playing and Myla doing silks.

"Yeah, they requested a partner act to open the party and ambient the rest of the time. You two up for working on a partner piece? Maybe in contortion straps?" she offered.

I looked at Myla, whose face didn't convey at all that she wanted that. "Why can't Jess and Ozzie do it? They already have a duo piece together," Myla spluttered out. I tried not to take it too personally, Myla was going through her own stuff, but I desperately wanted to resolve this tension that lingered between us.

"We aren't available that day," Ozzie said.

"Having a duo act in your back pocket is great. You can do straps, Myla. You're strong enough," Logan said, like it was the obvious answer.

"We don't have to do it if you don't want to, but I promise you can. It would be lovely to make a piece with you, Myla." I tried to soothe her, and she looked at me for what felt like the first time in months but was really only days.

I saw the vulnerability in her eyes of learning a new apparatus and having fear it wouldn't go well. Myla was truly lovely on silks. But her confidence in herself and who she was had been rocked with her breakup and her queerness. She was vulnerable to change, and this was a big one.

"If you say so," she whispered.

"Do you all mind if I talk to Myla privately for a moment?" I looked at the others, and they all mumbled they were going out to get some coffee anyway. They left, and Myla had a look of terror on her face as they all exited.

"Hey." I walked toward her, wanting to reach out and soothe her, but I kept my hands to myself.

She swallowed. "Hey."

"Want to talk about why you've been avoiding me?" I asked gently.

"I don't know what to do with my feelings for you. It feels like they came in like a tidal wave and smacked me on my ass. And we live together. I don't want you to go anywhere. I'm terrified about messing this up if we add something more to the mix, you know? And straps freaking terrify me," she blurted out quickly.

"How about we try to navigate it together, and then maybe you can stop avoiding me? And you can do straps, I promise. New things are scary, but you are capable." I stepped closer to her.

"Okay."

"How about a date?" I asked.

"A date?" she squeaked out, tilting her head to the side.

"Yes. A date. With me." I pointed to myself and gave her a cheeky smirk.

"Okay. Sure, one date to see what happens." She looked down and fiddled with her hands.

I grabbed them and gave her a gentle squeeze.

"It will be fun," I purred in her ear, and she shivered.

"Whatever doesn't kill you makes you stronger," she grumbled.

Myla had no idea the lengths I would go to show her how good we could be together, but she would soon see there was little I wouldn't do to win her over.

SEVENTEEN
MYLA

Dani stood in front of me, looking fantastic in black joggers and a cropped white tank with some sneakers. Their strong, compact body was hard to look away from. I had the sudden urge to run my fingers across the shaved part of their scalp and let my hand trail to their choppy waves on the other side.

"Hi," I said. "Is this okay?" I looked down at my jeans and cropped baby tee.

"You look great, Myla." Dani reached for my hand, and I took it. Butterflies erupted in my belly. They led me out to the car, and we hopped in.

"So are you going to tell me what we're doing, or is this all going to be a surprise?" I tried not to sneak too many looks at them as they drove. Before, I felt like I barely let my gaze linger on them, too afraid of the emotions it brought up in my belly. But now that we were giving this dating thing a go, it was like my walls were down. I could admire their olive-toned skin and the slashes carved out of their dark brows. Their impossibly long eyelashes framing dark-green eyes. It was like every part of them was calling to all parts of me.

"It's a surprise, if that's okay?" Dani looked at me, their gaze piercing mine.

"I like surprises, so I'm cool with it."

"It's a classic, quintessential date night, if you will." Dani smirked.

"What does that even mean?" I scrunched up my nose.

"You'll see," they said. I decided to relax as I enjoyed the ride.

I couldn't remember the last time I had been excited about a date. Certainly the ones I'd had thus far were not ones to remember, and it had been months since Jake and I had done anything like this.

There had been a time in our relationship when he'd really stepped up and we'd both planned fun adventures for one another. But that felt like years ago. Had it really been that long that we had been disconnected? Why hadn't I ended things sooner and not wasted my freaking time? Looking back, there were many times I had been disappointed or upset, but I'd shoved it down thinking it was best not to start a fight. When had I lost my voice? And why had I not been able to see that until now?

"Myla?" Dani asked with concern in their voice.

I blinked myself back to reality and out of the doom spiral that was happening in my brain.

"Yes?" I said, looking at them.

"Where'd you go?" They gently laced our fingers together, and I looked down at our intertwined hands. Our calluses pressed together, and our palms seem to be like two perfect puzzle pieces snuggling against one another.

"Just thinking about how dating has never been fun. I can't remember the last time I felt any excitement toward dating. But today feels different, so thank you for that." I looked into their eyes and smiled shyly. No more hiding what was on my mind or heart. The people who cared for me wanted to hear what I wanted. They wanted to listen, and Dani was no different.

"We're here." They gestured with their hands, and I finally looked around.

"We're going bowling?" I gasped excitedly.

"Yeah. A classic, right?" They grinned at me, and we got out of the car.

"I will have you know I'm an excellent bowler," I bragged.

"Ah, well, I will have you know I'm absolutely terrible." They waggled their brows at me.

"My years of being in a bowling league as a child have prepared me for this exact moment to kick your butt!" I shoved them playfully.

"A league?!" Dani asked.

"Yes, my parents thought it was an opportunity for me to meet kids outside of their circus community, and what do you know? I was a star," I teased. It was one of my favorite childhood memories. No matter where we had been, there was always a place to go bowling, and my parents had always done goofy throws like walking on their hands and nudging the ball. It had always been a hit wherever we'd gone.

"Myla, is this a competitive streak you have? Combat via bowling?" Dani said, tone teasing.

"Yes, yes it is. I take bowling very seriously," I murmured in their ear as we made our way in. "It's been years since I've bowled, but I'm sure I can still show off some skill here."

Dani laughed as we ordered some food to share and headed to our lane. I bowled first and got a strike. Brushing off my shoulder, I sauntered over to where Dani was sitting with a look of pure joy.

"Impressed yet?" I stood right in between their widespread legs. They pulled me down roughly on their thigh, and I yelped, my cheeky confidence flying out of me.

"I'm always impressed with you, Myla," they whispered in

my ear, their breath tickling my cheek. My chest expanded rapidly, and my heart felt like it could jump right out of my chest. Flirty Dani was absolutely devastating to my senses, and I kind of loved it. There was a confidence in them that made me want to purr on their lap.

"Better go take my turn." They stood up, and I slid off their lap in a heated mess.

"Now I'm going to be flustered for my turn!" I shouted as they threw an absolute garbage gutter ball. They looked like they didn't give a damn that they sucked.

I hit another strike, and then it was my turn to make them all hot and bothered.

"See, now it's my turn." I trailed my fingers across their arms, and they zeroed their gaze on me.

"Your turn?" Their voice dipped low.

"Yes." I walked up behind them as they stood to take their turn and wrapped my body around them.

"Ah…" They breathed out as I pressed harder into them.

"Like this." I guided their arm through the throw, and together we hit a couple of pins, but Dani didn't seem to care. Their eyes trailed down my face and landed on my lips.

"Myla, this isn't fair." They leaned in closer so our mouths were millimeters away.

"I don't know what you're talking about," I murmured, and then stepped back. Their eyes were blown wide, and their mouth opened in a little *o*. Two could play this flirty little game. Dani made me feel wanted and desired. It made my confidence soar, and I felt powerful every time my touch sent them into overdrive.

"You tease!" they accused as I sashayed away, swinging my hips and plopping back into my seat before sipping on my drink.

"We will just have to see about that later, now won't we," I said, and their gaze turned scorching.

The rest of the date was easy and carefree as we bowled a couple of games, and conversation flowed easily. Dani was already someone I felt comfortable with. I just hadn't fully given myself time and permission to be attracted to them. Men were easier to wrap my head around, and I felt inexperienced with everyone else. It had been hard for me to distinguish what I was feeling around them. When you grew up convincing yourself that the only people deserving of love and romantic attraction were men, it's hard to know how to distinguish those feelings with other people. All I knew is, with Dani, I felt effervescent, like I could float away on a happy, sparkly bubble with each of their smiles and touches making me warm and soft.

We abandoned our bowling lane and headed over to the arcade, where Dani absolutely kicked my butt at every single game we played. Payback was a hard pill to swallow.

"Why are you good at this?" I groaned as I failed miserably at Pac-Man for what felt like the tenth time. My fingers could not move fast enough, and my reaction time was absolutely trash.

"Why are you good at bowling?" they shot back. "I bet you were adorable in your bowling league. I would have loved to see little Myla strutting her stuff on these lanes."

"Yeah, the matching collared shirts were really something." I giggled thinking of how, at one point for my birthday, I'd wanted my parents and I to have matching shirts, and, of course, they'd obliged. They loved to encourage creativity and silliness. I'm sure I still had that hideous shirt somewhere.

"How are you feeling so far?" Dani asked as I attempted to play pinball.

"Feeling about what?"

"This?" Dani gestured between the two of us.

"Good, I think. I, I...just have no experience outside of men, so I may need some guidance if this gets more physical." I stammered a little, not used to feeling like I didn't know what to do or say in terms of intimacy. What if I was tragically bad in bed with Dani? They were probably, like, some amazing sex god in bed, if their easy and calm confidence was anything to go off of. I was nervous and shy when I was naked. My pleasure had always been put on the backburner with sex; my goal was to always try and make my partner feel good with little regard for myself. How messed up was that? I didn't even know where to unpack all that.

"Every person is different. And we'll get through it if we get there." Dani wrapped their arm around my waist. It sent heat straight to my center.

"I mean, I want to, I just feel like a scared teenager again trying out their first kiss, you know?" Relationships were already terrifying, and now, adding this new layer, I felt like a total dork. Everything was jumbled up inside me, and I didn't know how to get it all untangled.

"We've already had our first kiss, and the rest is easy." They placed a heated kiss on my neck, and I wiggled my thighs together.

"That's not fair. I can't focus on my game," I whined as my ball fell through.

"Sorry. I'll leave you alone then, darling." Dani went to step away, but I grabbed them before they got too far.

"Hmm, or we could get out of here?" I wanted to see what things were like with Dani. But I was intimidated. I didn't want to mess things up. But this was Dani. Kind, sweet, caring Dani. They wouldn't make me feel bad or ashamed in any way. They were safe.

"Is that what you want?" They slowly walked me backward until my back was against the wall and we were tucked into a small space, fully covered by the video games around us.

"Yes." I looked into their eyes as their hands ran up and

down my arms. I shivered under their touch as they landed with their palm on the back of my neck.

"How's this?" They rubbed their thumb along my jawline, and I swallowed.

"Really great," I whispered as they stepped into me and pressed their body against mine.

"And this?" They leaned and kissed the corner of my mouth.

"Jesus," I mumbled, thinking I would spontaneously combust from the tension in my body, even though we had barely done anything.

"Answer me, Myla," they commanded softly. It heated every part of my skin. Dani disarmed me, and I was putty in their hands.

"Y-yes. It feels good," I managed to get out in a breathy tone. My back naturally arched as I pressed myself further into them.

"Good." They pressed their lips to mine. Soft at first, sliding their tongue along the seam of my mouth as I sighed into them, wrapping my arms around their waist and wanting to feel every piece of them against every piece of me.

Then the intensity shifted as their mouth became fervent on my own. We kissed one another like we were starved, grabbing and grinding against each other. It was the single sexiest thing I had been a part of in years, and at a bowling alley no less.

Dani broke away first, panting. "Let's go back to the house." They pulled me along, and I felt dizzy with desire.

"Yeah, let's do that." I couldn't think of anything else I would rather do more.

EIGHTEEN
DANI

I could tell Myla was a bit nervous, but damn she was enthusiastic. We got back to the house, and our hands were all over one another, exploring and touching. I grabbed her palm and led her back to what was now our bed. The thought sent a possessive thrill through me.

She bit her lip as I gently closed the door and sat her down on the duvet. Her purple hair was messy and her cheeks flushed.

"You're extraordinary, Myla," I praised as I started to gently strip off my clothes. I watched her eyes travel across my body. Her eyes lingered on my pierced nipples, then dipped lower as I slid off my pants.

"So are you, Dani," she panted as I stepped in between her legs and widened them.

"I know this is all new. Talk to me when something feels good and when something doesn't. Use your words as we play with one another," I said as I kissed along her jaw, and her head fell back. She swallowed and nodded her head.

"Words, beautiful," I mumbled against her neck where I bit softly, and she groaned. Myla may not have been able to say what she wanted before, but with me, I wanted to pull every delicious, wicked thing out of her mind and then use it to bring her pleasure again and again. There would be no hiding from me when we were in the bedroom together. Soon I would know her inside and out, and she would be begging me with her deepest desires.

"Yes. I will use my words," she said, and I pulled away, reaching for the hem of her shirt and looking at her.

"Can I take this off?"

"Yes." Her pupils swallowed me whole as I gently removed her top to reveal a lacy bra underneath. I wanted to run my fingertips along the smooth swell of her breasts, but that could wait. This experience would undoubtedly set the tone for her queer relationships, and I selfishly wanted it to be the best one she ever had.

"I get regularly tested for STIs, and my last tests were all negative. Have you been tested since you and Jake were together?" My tone was light, but it was important to me to set the tone of what the bare minimum should be between partners, because I had little faith that Myla's previous experiences would have done the same.

"Yes, I have. Thank you for telling me," Myla whispered, licking her lips. Nodding, I continued my perusal of her glorious body.

"You can touch me too, Myla," I said as I took her in, and her hesitant fingers reached out and touched my skin, trailing along my arms and along my ribs. Her fingertips caressed my nipples, playing with the bars there. I shuddered beneath her touch. God, I wanted her mouth everywhere, sucking and tugging on every fucking part of me.

"How about these? Can I take these off?" I tugged at her pants, and she nodded as she lay back. I peeled them off, revealing a matching lacy thong. It nearly took my breath away.

She blushed as I took her in. "I wanted to impress you, if we, uh... did this." She stumbled over her words. What a magnificent thing she was.

"Oh, I'm impressed, and the matching set is just icing on the cake." I kissed along her hip bones and licked up her ribs. Her hands were balled into fists as I found all the spots on her body that made her groan and arch off the bed. Her reaction to my touch just made my desire grow. She was beautifully responsive, every groan and moan a little cue to where my girl liked to be touched and caressed.

"Do you like this, Myla?" I purred as I sucked at her inner thigh.

"Yes, Dani. More. Please. I want more," she panted. Her panties were absolutely soaked. My arousal was gathering on my thighs, and so badly I wanted to grab her hand and guide her there, but that could wait. Right now, I wanted to savor every little wriggle of her body as I took her higher and higher.

"Can this come off?" I pulled on her thong.

"Yes, and my bra. Please, Dani, touch my tits. I feel like I might combust if you don't," she mumbled, her eyes tightly closed. Smiling at her request, I stilled my hands.

"I will, but you have to look at me, darling," I said, and her eyes flew open as I pulled her up and gently brought my fingertips to the clasp on her bra. "That's a good girl."

Her eyes went wide, and a blush crept on her cheeks from the praise. It stroked something deep within me. Her breasts fell into my hands and looked absolutely delicious. I tossed the fabric to the side and palmed both of them, squeezing tightly as she sighed.

My mouth was salivating as I pulled one of her stiff peaks into my mouth and sucked gently.

"Dani," she groaned, bucking into me as I gave attention to the other one.

"Does that feel good, Myla?" I pushed her back down gently, and her eyes were heavy with lust.

"Yes. This is, like, the best and longest foreplay I've ever had," she mused.

"Oh, Myla, we're just getting started. I could play with you all night." I made my way down to her mouthwatering pussy. I spread her legs wide and kneeled between her thighs.

"Prop up on your elbows and watch, Myla," I commanded, and she did without hesitation, her tits on full display as she gazed down at me with a small grin on her lips.

"I had a dream about you doing this," she confessed as I trailed my mouth along the length of her muscular thighs.

"A dream? What did I do to you in this dream?" The fact Myla had dreamed of this had me practically melting.

"You ate me out and gave me the most earth-shattering orgasm I've ever had. I didn't even think to watch it like this, but I... I think I really like seeing you between my thighs," she said, biting her lip.

"Good, because I'm planning on spending a lot of time down here." And with that, I dove into her wet folds, taking one long swipe of my tongue against her wetness and savoring the taste of her. God, I could drown in her scent. I sucked at her clit and worshiped her pretty pussy. She was glorious, writhing underneath me and chanting my name.

Licking and lapping, I worked her clit and slid one finger in, then gently added another, wanting her to feel all of me. My arousal was growing as I tongue-fucked her. Her hips moved in time to my thrusts, and my tongue swirled around her bundle of nerves. Her legs began to shake, and she plunged her hands into my hair as she threw her head back and arched deeper into me.

"Dani!" she yelled as I felt her thighs squeeze around me as she came in a rush of liquid on my mouth and hands. She trembled as I pushed her through her own waves of ecstasy, her hips rocking against me and her whimpering echoing through the room.

"How was that?" I said, crawling up her body.

"Amazing, much better than my dream, Dani," she said as I leaned down and kissed her, wanting her to taste how delicious she was on my tongue. We collided together, her gripping my back and running her fingernails down my spine. Myla wrapped her legs around me so her wetness pressed against my skin.

"Dani, I want to make you come. Will you tell me how? Please?" She searched my face with such earnestness. I tucked her hair behind her ear and thought of nothing I would like more than to teach Myla how to make me scream.

"Yes, Myla. It's your turn to get between my legs."

She beamed as I rolled off of her, and she scampered to stand and then kneel between my legs, my wetness sliding down my thighs.

"Okay, will you tell me how you like it?" she asked shyly. Myla's eyes stayed glued to mine as she kissed and nibbled my inner thighs and then up to my hip bones, licking and sucking her way across my skin. Her fingertips danced close to my folds, but she looked unsure. Grabbing her fingers, I guided her to my clit and showed her what I liked. Gently, I released her hand, and she swallowed, licking her lips as she brought her fingers to her mouth and sucked. She was the single sexiest person I had ever met.

"Can I...?" She settled herself right at my entrance, and I widened my legs. Nodding, she gave a tentative kiss on my thigh before I settled my hands on her head and brought her mouth closer to where I needed her. Groaning, I ground against her as her tongue hesitantly moved, and she got bolder the more I encouraged her.

"Good girl, Myla, right there. Now add a finger," I purred as she enthusiastically followed each of my commands, swiping with her tongue and pumping in and out of me. She was an excellent listener, eager to take all my guidance. Her hot, wet mouth and fingers were sending me over the edge as she continued to look at me with those big, beautiful eyes.

"Ahhh, Myla," I yelled as she continued, and I came in a rush of pleasure licking against my spine and spreading all the way to my fingertips and toes. I pinched my nipples hard and sighed as she continued to lick and suck, taking me all the way through each crescendo of pleasure.

"Did I do okay?" She sat back on her heels and looked at me shyly, her face glistening with my orgasm.

"You did great, Myla," I said as she crawled back up and took her time laying open-mouthed kisses across my belly and ribs. Her mouth closed around my piercings, and I nearly came undone again as the pleasure and pain wrapped into one beautiful sensation. By the time she had given every inch of my body her mouth, I was desperate for her lips on mine again, so I guided her up.

We kissed and explored one another by touching and feeling. Myla practically purred every time I said "good girl" and told her what to do. Our bodies molded perfectly together as we tried to memorize every inch of one another.

Eventually we snuggled into one another and sighed, our naked bodies fitting together quite well.

"I like when you call me a good girl." She blushed, trailing her hands against my arms.

"Oh, I can tell," I teased.

"Stop it! I didn't even know I liked that. But when you tell me what to do and then praise me... It's very sexy." She bit her lip and looked into my eyes. Her vulnerability in this moment was something I wanted to cherish and hold in my hands forever.

"I just had a feeling. I like when you obey my commands. It's a huge turn on," I said, stroking her hair.

"That was… That was unlike anything I've ever experienced. Thank you for taking care of me tonight, Dani." She pulled our hands together and tugged them to her chest.

"I really like you, Myla," I said, scooting closer to her, our noses practically touching.

"I like you too. Do you think we could go on another date and do this again?"

"Would I like to spend more time with you and get you naked and squirming underneath me again?" I asked.

Myla's mouth dropped open in a shocked *o*.

"Yes. I would."

"Okay, I have another request." She smirked mischievously at me.

"And what is that?" I raised an eyebrow.

"Can we go to the shelter tomorrow and pick our little pet?" She was giddy with excitement. We hadn't been able to do it since I moved in, and getting a pet together was a huge step that I wasn't sure either of us were ready for.

"Are you sure you want to get an animal with me?" I asked softly. I didn't want things to get too intense too fast.

"Yes. Dani, you were my friend first, and now something more? I'm not worried about us. Are you?" Myla said seriously.

"No, I'm not. But we just started this, so I want to take as much time as both of us need. However, let's go look at some animals, and then you decide what you want and I will be here to help you care for them." I drew a finger down her jaw, and she shivered. That seemed like the best compromise I could come up with.

"Okay." She snuggled in deeper and closed her eyes.

I wrapped my arms around her and sighed. I hoped she was in it for the long haul, because I didn't know how I could let her go after having her once already.

NINETEEN
MYLA

The rows of dogs and cats in the shelter seemed to go on forever, and I couldn't help but want to take each and every one of them home. Dani was chatting with the front desk person about some more information, and I continued to prowl up and down looking at all their sad little faces. It broke my heart, but I knew this was better than on the streets. Their best chance of finding a forever home was through these shelters, but their cages still made me sad.

There were very clear divisions of cats and dogs, and I wasn't sure which one I wanted. Growing up, I didn't get to have either, because my parents were always on and off show tours, so it was hard for us to commit to a pet.Oddly, there was one stall where a puppy and kitty were together. They curled into one another like they were one giant fluff ball instead of two separate animals. I looked around for a worker and didn't see anyone. Squatting down, I pressed myself close to the glass to get a better look. Slowly, the two furballs untangled themselves, and I could get a better look at their adorable little faces.

It was a small black cat with the cutest little splash of white across its chest and a small white puppy who sort of looked naked with its fine hair and light-brown ears. They took one look at me, and in a flash, they were huddled together again as if they couldn't bear to be parted from one another's sides. Maybe they had been found together and couldn't be separated.

Quickly, I walked back to where Dani was still chatting with the front desk person and inserted myself into the conversation.

"Hi, the kennel that has the puppy and the kitty. Are they a bonded pair or something?" I asked, tapping my fingers on the front desk.

"Let me look," she said, clicking away at her computer.

"Did you find any that you like?" Dani asked gently.

I blushed, thinking about our night last night and how this morning Dani had gotten up and made breakfast and brought it to bed. I wasn't used to being treated this way. It was lovely, and I had too many emotions swirling around in my heart that I wasn't sure what to do with them all. Dani was a service-oriented person, and it was wild to me that they would want to do all this for me just because they cared. Now, here we were pet shopping together even though they would technically be mine and Dani would be helping. An image of us playing house forever flashed into my head, our little furballs playing while we snuggled up on the couch. In my head, things got heated, just like they had last night, and my thighs clenched together.

Dani raised their brows at me like they could hear my thoughts, and it made me blush even harder.

"It looks like they just came in, and they are bonded together. Both of them are set to be fixed soon, and then they will be ready to adopt as soon as they're recovered," she answered politely.

"Can I meet them?" Clearing my throat, I tried to look anywhere other than Dani's smirking face. Their eyes seem to caress my skin just like their touch did, and I had to hold back my body's reaction to them.

"Sure! Let me get you set up in a room." She hustled away, and I continued to avoid Dani's gaze. If I looked at them long enough, I was sure I would spontaneously combust from the horny thoughts racing through my brain.

"Why are you blushing, Myla?" Dani whispered in my ear, and I nearly jumped out of my skin. Clearly, everything was written across my face. I wasn't very good at hiding my emotions from them, not that I was trying too hard.

"No reason," I murmured.

"It wouldn't have anything to do with the things we were doing last night, would it?" they asked me, stepping closer into my space.

It's more like I was daydreaming about when it could happen again and how often we could do it moving forward.

"Uh." I looked around, but no one else at the shelter was paying us any attention. Was this really the place to get into this? What if someone heard me blurt out all my Dani-riddled fantasies? Oddly, it didn't turn me off as much as I thought, and instead made my insides turn to liquid heat.

"Or what happened when we both woke up in the middle of the night?" Dani was invading my space, their mischievous green eyes scanning my face. All I could see, smell, and hear was them. Their clean, earthy scent seemed to wrap around me, yet I still found myself wanting to lean in and inhale against their skin. My heart felt like it would nearly explode out of my chest from the way their gaze seemed to consume me. Blinking, I tried to shake myself out of this sexy-induced haze, and they chuckled.

"Dani!" I hissed, pushing them in the shoulder as they snickered harder. That was another first—waking up in the middle of the night and having another mind-blowing orgasm, then falling straight back to bed. Who was I becoming? This was more sex than I'd had in the last year or so.

"What? I'm just trying to understand where your head's at." They placed a gentle kiss on my cheek that sent my heart fluttering.

"We've got you all set up!" The woman came back, and Dani grabbed my hand, pulling me along. Their fingers fit perfectly in mine, and it seemed like the most natural thing in the world.

We followed her back to a play room where the small kitten and puppy were squished together once again.

"Right now, the puppy's name is Biscuit and the cat's name is Brownie," she said.

"Cute." Dani plopped down on the floor and grabbed a few toys to try and entice them to come over to us.

"Both females. If you have any questions, let me know, and just come out when you're done." She closed us in, and I sat down next to Dani.

The kitten became curious first and slowly left little Biscuit's side to sniff at Dani's fingers. The woman had left some treats for us to try to hand out to them. Little Brownie tentatively chewed on one, then gobbled it up.

"See, wasn't that yummy?" Dani cooed at the cat, and it slowly crawled into their lap. It took no time at all for the little cat to start purring as Dani scratched behind its ears. The sight of this small animal seeking refuge in Dani's strong thighs did something unexpected to my low belly.

Get it together, Myla. One night of sex, and you can't keep anything in your pants?

Clearing my throat, I tried to wiggle my way over to the little pup. Biscuit seemed to perk up in curiosity, but still wouldn't move from her little ball in the corner.

Brownie abandoned Dani, walking back over to Biscuit and gently batting at her ear.

"This is adorable. Do you want to come and play, little ones?" I jingled some toys and squeaked a few plushies until both of them came over and sniffed my hands.

I held out a treat to each one, and Biscuit gobbled hers up with a goofy little grin on her face. It didn't take long for both of them to be running around our laps and jumping over each other as they played and leaped about, hungry for our attention and excited to be entertained by new stuffies.

"They're really cute," Dani mused as they tumbled with one another across the floor.

"I think I want both of them." My heart melted at the sight of them. There was no way I would be able to choose between the two of them, and they were besties. They had to be adopted together.

"If that's what you want, I'll support you all the way." Dani squeezed my knee.

"Are you ready to become a parent of two?" I teased. Dani rolled their eyes.

"With you? Sure, why not."

I snapped lots of pictures and videos of the two of them and sent them to the group text of all our friends.

Myla: Who wants to help take care of a kitten and a puppy?

The texts came fast and furious as everyone freaked out about the little animals.

Logan: MEEEEEEE.
Jess: If I have to.
Ozzie: They are so stinking cute!
Bex: I'm a great babysitter.
Aven: Say less.

"Can we take a picture together?" I asked Dani.

"Sure." They scooted closer to me and wrapped their arms around me as I snapped a selfie. I looked at it and fought the flutter in my belly. They were breathtaking at any moment, but in this photo together, we looked good. A perfect pair.

"You sure you won't leave my house now that I might be adopting these two?" I asked seriously.

"Myla, it's going to take a lot more for me to leave your house, and you, than a pair of adorable animals," they said seriously as Brownie and Biscuit jumped into their lap and playfully snarled and swatted at one another.

"Okay, let's go get the adoption person then." I stood up and left the room to find the receptionist and ask her about what could be done.

Quickly, I found out I would have to wait a few more weeks, but I could put a hold on them for adoption.

"Absolutely. Whatever I need to make sure I can take them home with me is perfectly fine," I said.

I went through the logistics, and I could come back in a few weeks. Once they had vaccinations and were fixed, they could come home with me. With us.

Tearfully, we said goodbye to the pair and left the shelter.

"Sorry we couldn't take them home today. But soon!" Dani gripped my hand in theirs as we walked back to the car.

"Me too. But they will be home soon. Should we go to the pet store?" I asked.

"Let's do it."

The rest of the day, we felt like a totally normal couple shopping for our first fur babies together, even though I would technically be the one adopting them. Dani and I had only just slept together. Trying not to overthink it, I distracted myself by brainstorming toy ideas and if we wanted to give them new names.

In some ways, it felt like Dani had been there all along and it just took me ages to realize and be comfortable with us being together. The ease we had with one another was lovely, and I found myself wanting nothing more than to get back to the house and do something about it. But was this too much, too soon? It felt like a natural progression, and one we were going to do anyway before sex got added to the equation.

"Dani?" I asked as we drove back to the house.

"Yes, Myla?" they asked.

"I really like you."

The corners of their mouth ticked up. "And I really like you."

"And when we get back to the house, I would like to show you," I said, dropping my voice. And I swear they drove a little faster. But I kept my promise, showing Dani again and again how much I liked them with my whole body.

TWENTY

DANI

We walked into the bar hand and hand. It felt good to show Myla was mine, and I was hers. She looked amazing in a purple dress that matched her hair and platform sandals. Logan, Bex, and Ozzie were already at the table. I imagined Aven and Jess were not far away. Our Cirque Callisto family was often fluttering around one another, and it felt good to have these people around me.

"Congrats, Ozzie!" Myla gave Ozzie a squeeze.

"Sling-free, bitches!" Ozzie punched her arms out in rapid fire.

"Yeah, but you aren't cleared for all the aerial and circus stuff, so slow down, Oz." Logan scowled at her, eyeing the way she had just flapped her arms about.

"You're getting very mother-hen in your thirties, Lo," Myla teased and squeezed in next to her. I sat right next to her in the booth.

"Hey, as someone who has performed with quite a few circus companies, I can tell you Logan is one of the best, safest, and caring directors I've ever worked with. She's the glue that holds us together, and I'm really grateful to be under your watch and mentorship." I settled my hand on Myla's bare thigh and watched as a slow blush crept up on her cheeks. God she was responsive. It was delicious.

"Thank you, Dani. They get it! Everyone can get off my ass for being such a rule follower about safety, because it's meant to keep all you assholes safe." She death-stared each one of us down.

"This asshole is grateful for you too." Bex leaned over and placed a kiss on her cheek.

"I knew you were my favorite," she teased, and we all made a fuss about it at the table while Logan cackled.

Aven and Jess appeared with a tray full of drinks and snacks from the bar.

"Alright, everyone grab something to drink and let's make a toast," Jess commanded as we each plucked something from the tray.

"To Ozzie's recovery and her being sling-free!" Jess held her glass up, and we hooped and hollered as we clinked glasses and took sips. My heart felt full with this new family I had. There was a rightness here I had never experienced outside of Soaren and Lily.

"Okay, but serious question..." Aven placed her drink down and folded her hands in front of her. Her solemn expression made me want to squirm a little.

"What?" Myla's eyebrows went up like she was nervous.

"Are you two dating?" She batted her eyelashes innocently. The question hit me in the chest, and I fought a loud exhale. I wanted Myla to answer the question, because I was more than comfortable telling people we were dating. There was no one else for me right now, and I had a hard time imagining there would be anyone as lovely, kind, and intelligent as this woman in front of me. I didn't know if we were comfortable calling one another each other's partners, but we were definitely dating and being exclusive about it in my heart.

"Well..." Myla's blush deepened. She looked at me hopelessly, and I gave in, desperately wanting to come to her rescue.

"Yes?" I replied, taking my arm from her thigh to the backs of her shoulders. Myla nodded and smiled, like she'd needed me to say it first.

"Yes," Myla parroted, the corner's of her mouth tipping up.

"Who asked out whom?" Logan said in a serious tone.

"Technically, it was me," I replied.

"*Ha*, you owe me ten bucks." Logan had a smirk on her face directed at Ozzie.

"Damnnit," Ozzie grumbled, pulling out her phone to Venmo her.

"You all had a bet going? On what?!" Myla's jaw dropped open. Everyone had felt the tension between us in the weeks past, except maybe Myla. The thought made me giggle.

"How long it would take before you two were going to try things out. I bet you would ask first, Myla, and Logan bet it would be Dani," Ozzie replied.

"You all didn't want in on the bet?" I asked Jess, Aven, and Bex, rolling my eyes at how invested everyone was in our relationship.

"I mean, I didn't make an official bet, but I was with Ozzie." Jess took another sip of her cocktail, looking as inconspicuous as she could.

Aven snickered. "I was team Dani for sure!"

"Bex?" I raised my brow at him.

"I was just here for the show," he said. Of course Bex would take the middle.

"Isn't this cute, though. Two circus couples. God, I'm not only an amazing director, performer, and overall human being, but also a bona fide matchmaker." Logan dabbed away imaginary tears. "Someone give me an award or something. I would like to thank all the people in my life for being horny romantics..."

Myla rolled her eyes. "God help us."

"Two couples does not a matchmaker make," Bex teased, pinching her arm.

"Ah, but who said I'm stopping at two?" Logan purred, and we all pointedly looked at Aven, who choked on her drink and avoided Bex's piercing gaze. Logan was not subtle, and she seemed unbothered by both their reactions.

"Anyway..." Jess said, trying to bring the conversation away from the obvious tension in the air. Bex had a shit-eating grin on his face, while Aven tried to recover by drowning in her margarita.

"Who's ready for our large gig tomorrow? All hands on deck doesn't happen very often, except at our own shows, of course, but for a personal party, it's nearly unheard of." Logan tapped her long fingernails on the table.

"I mean, I'm ready to get paid and look hot." Ozzie gave us a little shimmy, and Jess rolled her eyes. She had been itching to get back to it. The hardest part of recovery was always waiting until you were truly ready to go, not just when you got tired of it.

"You're grounded, Oz. That's all you are doing, got it?" Logan took on her authoritative tone again.

"I'll keep her in line," Jess answered.

"Oh my god," Myla whispered next to me. Her body froze next to me, and I immediately wanted to soothe whatever was making her body go into fight-or-flight mode.

"What?" I asked.

"Jake," she hissed, and I swore everyone at the table whipped their heads around at once to see him striding into the bar with a couple other guys. *Fucking Jake.*

"Do you want to leave?" Ozzie asked, like she was ready to go to battle for Myla.

"No, it's fine. Maybe he won't even notice us over here. No worries. What were you saying, Logan?" Myla tried to settle into a cool gaze, but the anxiety was rolling off her in waves. Her foot tapped erratically underneath the table, and she picked at her nails.

Logan looked at her hard and pursed her lips. "The gig tomorrow will have a few patrons who have asked about us performing for a few events this upcoming year, but want to see us in action at a large-scale event. We will want to put our best foot forward."

"Shit, he's coming over here." Jess scowled as he strutted over to the table with a few of his presumed friends in tow. Our previous conversation slipped away as he walked over.

"Myla. It's nice to see you out." Jake slurred slightly, like he was already on his way to intoxication. His body swayed slightly, and I swore he was about ten seconds from face-planting onto our table.

Myla just looked at him and said nothing, her eyes wide. Why had he even bothered to come over here? What could he possibly think to accomplish by antagonizing her? The rage in me turned my eyes into daggers, and I wanted to launch myself at him if he attempted to come any closer.

"Don't you have anything to say to me? Just could kick a man out of his own house?" He leaned heavily on the table, and his friends behind him snickered. It took everything in me not to bear my teeth at him. I was small in stature, but you didn't do what I did as a performer without muscles to back it up. Plus, I was scrappy as heck, and growing up with a brother made me very prepared to take this prick down, especially if he was this drunk.

Myla's eyes went glassy, and her big, beautiful orbs locked on mine like a plea for help.

"Last time I checked, you didn't own anything. Myla owns the house, and you couldn't be bothered to pay rent."

The words tumbled out of my mouth before I could stop myself. My arm tightened around her shoulder, and his eyes caught the movement, zeroing in on where our skin touched.

"What, are you two dating now or something?" Jake looked between the two of us, anger filling his eyes.

"Jake, I suggest you back away from this table before I get your sorry ass escorted out of here," Logan purred, her tone absolutely lethal as she slowly rose from the table.

His friends behind him looked taken aback by Logan's harsh words, but Jake was too focused on my arm around Myla. His eyes seemed to focus and then unfocus, like he couldn't tell what was real and what was the alcohol sloshing in his brain.

"Was this your plan all along? You were already cheating on me, and then you kicked me out!" He slammed his hands on the table. Jess and Aven stood up and forced him to back away from us. Their hands wrapped around his shoulders, making him take a few steps away from the table.

"It doesn't matter what or whom she was doing. You need to leave and never think about Myla again. Do you under-stand, Jake, or do you need us to spell it out for you?" Aven crossed her arms over her chest as his friends scattered away, not looking for any sort of trouble. *Fucking cowards.*

Men always thought they could intimidate other people, and as soon as there was pushback, they fled like the roaches they were.

Unfortunately, Jake was incapable of moving his feet.

"But I love you." His face fell, and he started sobbing.

"No, no, no. We are not dealing with your fragile male tears. You need to leave, Jake. Hey, come back and get your friend now!" Jess yelled, and his friends scrambled over and took the blubbering Jake away, who kept moaning Myla's name.

"Are you okay?" I asked, looking to where Myla sat, still and silent.

"Yeah. I mean, I certainly wasn't expecting that, but I guess I was bound to run into him eventually. I'm glad you all were here with me." She wiped her eyes.

"Men are the worst," Bex said, sipping his drink.

"They really are," Logan added.

"Threatening to get his ass escorted out was nice. I'll have to remember that for next time..." Aven snickered.

"Next time? Who the hell are you getting into fights with these days?" Logan retorted. The mood lightened, and we were able to enjoy our time celebrating Ozzie as opposed to fielding any wild exes.

"Are you sure you're okay?" I pulled Myla in, and she leaned into me.

"Yeah, I don't want him around, but I don't want him like that either. That was uncomfortable to watch. Especially considering I used to date and love him. I don't know, it was weird, and I would love nothing more than to never see his stupid face again."

"We can totally make that happen," I said, running my fingertips across her bare skin.

"Thanks for being here." She leaned in and placed a soft kiss on my mouth.

"Ew, get a room," Aven teased.

I'd really love nothing more than that, but that could wait for later. Tonight, I was happy to be in the presence of all my friends and the girl I was falling in love with.

Twenty-One
Myla

The house was ready for the little fur babies, but we had to wait a little longer before they would be ready for us. I tried to distract myself by throwing my body into training. Things felt good right now.

Dani and I were dating and having frequent mind-blowing sex. New fur babies were coming into my home. Gigs were happening regularly, and I finally felt more settled after everything with Jake despite seeing him the other day. My body felt calm, and my house actually felt like a home, not just the place Jake and I used to live in together.

"You seem very happy." Jess nudged me with her shoulder while we practiced in the warehouse together. She twisted up her long, dark hair in a bun on top of her head and gave me a knowing look.

"I am. Things between Dani and me... They feel really good and easy in a way I didn't expect, you know? Life finally feels settled after the breakup." I grabbed a foam roller to work on my calves a little as we chatted.

"That's really good to hear," Aven said, plopping down beside me as Jess chalked her hands.

"We were worried about you. I'm glad you're feeling a little lighter these days," Jess added before she mounted her hoop.

"How are you and Ozzie?" I asked, and she talked while she lifted her toes to the bar.

"Really good. I love her a lot." Jess grinned through her reps and took on a dreamy, far-off look, like she was remembering all the reasons Ozzie was meant for her.

"And you?" I lifted one brow at Aven, who was stretching beside me.

"Me what?" Aven asked coyly.

"How's that strict no-dating thing going?" I knew it was digging into a sore spot of hers, but I worried about her keeping everything bottled up like that. One day, she would emotionally pop, and I hoped to god she would let us comfort her then.

Aven swallowed and pursed her lips. "Fine."

"Just fine?" Logan asked, sauntering in and beginning her warm-up on the trapeze like she hadn't been eavesdropping this whole time.

"Yeah, *fine*," Aven emphasized, trying to close down the conversation. "Dating sucks some major balls, which no one fucking likes." Her tone was rough and low.

"Right. Does that dating ban include a no sex or hookup ban, or is it just dating?" I said, leaning into her while she pointedly avoided my eyes. We had been gently poking and prodding at Aven to open up, but she had some firm walls up right now. If she couldn't open up to her best friends, then who could she count on? I wanted to be there for her like she had been there for me. They had all held me physically and emotionally through this whole thing with Jake, and I wouldn't have made it otherwise.

"We're not talking about me right now." Aven cleared her throat and lifted her head, planting a grimace on her face.

"We're talking about how lovely you and Dani are!" she shot back, slamming the door on that conversation for the hundredth time. I wouldn't push her anymore, but I so badly wanted to wrap her up in my arms and tell her I was here if she needed anything.

"Fine. I mean, there's nothing much to report. We're doing well, and we will get the fur babies soon! I'm really excited to have pets!" I clapped giddily.

"Jake was against it, wasn't he?" Logan asked through her shoulder shrugs.

"Yeah, just one of the *many* red flags I ignored. But I think it will be good to have little animals to take care of." I stood up and made my way over to the silks. There were many things I denied myself because Jake wasn't on board, and instead of standing up for myself, I just let it go. How much of myself had I sacrificed for him? How much of myself was lost while I tried to hold him together? It wasn't something I liked to think about.

It was even harder not to feel like I had just let it all happen. Yes, I played a part in us losing touch, but he wanted me to be small, and I deserved to take up more space.

"And you, Logan?" Aven said, pointedly rolling out her acro mat and slapping it against the floor.

"Me what?" Logan asked as she inverted on the bar and did some split drills.

"You're also in a no-dating situation. Does that include physicality for you?" Aven was fighting right back with her snarky tone, and Logan's eyes narrowed.

"Nothing has entered me except my battery-operated toys in quite some time, thank you very much. Now that I shared, you should share..." Logan trailed off, waiting for Aven to fill in the blanks, her eyes going wide waiting for Aven's retort. Logan was an open book, while Aven was a locked-up tomb. "You're not getting out of this conversation that easily. These bitches might let it go, but I won't. So... Spill. It," Logan practically commanded, and Aven's mouth dropped open. If anyone could crack her open, it was Lo. Jess and I looked back and forth between the two of them, waiting for Aven to respond.

Aven chewed her lip and sighed. "Fine, but it stays between the four of us. I mean it. Don't tell Ozzie or Dani!" Aven threw her finger around accusingly.

Jess rolled her eyes, and I smiled gently at her.

"*Spill,*" Logan demanded again, perching on her bar.

"Bex and I..." she started, then looked around as if someone were going to pop out of nowhere and say *gotcha*.

"No one else is here! Say it!" Jess shouted.

"Okay, Bex and I hooked up again after the drag show." Aven winced a little, like saying it out loud made it written in stone.

"Why are you wincing?! Who cares? That's amazing! Didn't you say before that Bex was like the best one-night stand you ever had?" I asked, a little confused. This felt like a good thing to me. Bex was lovely, and Aven needed someone who would show up for her no matter what.

"Yes, and this was even better than the last time..." Aven whined. "But we can't just be fuck buddies here!" She threw up her hands in frustration.

"And why not?" Logan asked, raising a brow.

"Because that makes everything more complicated. Friends with benefits never works out, and I don't want to date," Aven grumbled. She was her own worst enemy here. She was making up rules to protect herself, but it was only going to hurt her in the end.

"I mean, if you made up that rule for yourself, you could totally change it," Jess said casually while fiddling with her hands.

"But I don't want to! Every relationship I've had goes up

in a ball of fucking flames, and the common denominator is me! I can't do this with Bex, because I actually give a shit about him." Aven huffed, a sliver of vulnerability and truth finally coming out. My heart ached for her. She was wonderful. I just wished she would give herself the chance to feel her feelings.

"Aven," I said, and she shot a glare at me.

"Don't give me that pitying look, or I will flick you on the nose," she seethed, tucking away that moment like it had never even existed in the first place. I held up my hands in surrender, and the corners of her mouth ticked up.

"Alright, alright. No flicking please. Maybe just take it slow, day by day, and remember to go to therapy," Logan said, trying to lighten the mood.

"I've never not been in therapy," Aven mumbled, and I giggled.

"Everyone has relationship head-trash. It's okay if this is hard for you," I said lightly, trying not to get physically attacked by her flicking fingers.

"I know. It's just not something I want to deal with right now, so I'm avoiding it." Aven looked defeated from a battle she was constantly setting herself up to lose.

"Okay, if you say so." Logan dropped the subject, and we didn't speak of it anymore. I continued to go about my training and let my hopes soar high for the possibilities in front of me with Dani and our new little pets.

TWENTY-TWO
DANI

"It's Brownie and Biscuit time!" Myla squealed in the car. Her excitement was adorable. My heart wanted to explode with warmth every time I got to spend time with her. I was falling hard and fast. If I was being honest, it had been happening since I moved in. Things were only escalating in and outside of the bedroom. I was careening toward something I had never felt before.

"Did you decide if you want to keep the names or try out something else?" I asked as we pulled right and into the adoption center. I could practically feel her vibrating next to me. This was the first time I had seen her like this, and her joy made my heart swell.

She pursed her lips. "I wanted to change them at first, but Brownie and Biscuit are pretty cute. My little BBs."

"I can get behind the BBs." We walked into the shelter hand in hand. Like we were a true couple, picking up our little pets.

Myla went to work on double-checking all the paperwork and asking her final questions about what she needed at the house, even though she was incredibly prepared. We had been to the pet store several times since the adoption process had started, and she had done a ton of research on what they would need. Myla was already going to be the best pet parent I knew.

The process had been lovely, and it brought a special light to Myla that was contagious. My worries were wiggling around in my brain. God, I wanted to help her with them, but I was nervous to call them mine as much as hers. I didn't want to overstep the boundaries of our relationship. They were hers, and someday they could be mine too, but not yet. We had barely just begun, even though it felt like I had known her in my heart forever.

"Okay, wait just a few moments, and we will get them crated so you can take them home!" The receptionist hustled off as we sat in the lobby together.

My phone rang, and I saw it was the creative director I had worked with previously when I'd stayed with Soaren and Lily.

"That's weird." I hadn't heard from her in awhile, basically since I left. She would have no reason to contact me unless she had another opportunity to offer me. We had left on excellent terms. She promised she would keep in touch, as I was unsure of where I would be or if I would be back. At the time, nowhere had felt like it could possibly be a permanent place. But now things had changed. I had changed. Myla was here, and so were my friends. My new family. For the first time in my life, I felt steady and grounded with the choices I was making and the people around me.

"What?" Myla asked, glancing at my screen. My thoughts seemed to skitter off into a million different pieces. There was no need to hurtle toward assumptions when I had no idea what she wanted. It could be great. It could just be a check-in.

"It's an old creative director." I swallowed, unsure of why suddenly there was a huge lump in my throat. Why did I feel like I was getting called to the principal's office?

"You should answer it! What if it's some fancy-schmancy show or gig?" Myla nudged my shoulder, and I decided to finally pick up the call. Nothing had changed in this moment except I should just answer the damn phone and not be such a coward.

"Hey, Katie. How are you?" I asked in a scratchy voice.

"Dani! I'm excellent. How are you?" Her voice was light and twinkling. Katie always carried positive energy throughout the whole time I'd worked with her. Sometimes it was a little unsettling.

"Good. I'm surprised to hear from you." Scared was a better term. The reality was this call could rock the foundations I had built here. Why was that terrifying to me? Normally, I was a nomad, floating from place to place. Who had I become now that I'd met Myla and joined Cirque Callisto?

"I've got an opportunity for you. The headliner for the show I'm putting on in Vegas backed out at the last minute due to some health issues. And no one can handle the rigor of their performance except you... That is, if you still play instruments while you do straps?" she asked, her voice hopeful. My stomach plunged down to the floor. *Holy shit.*

I nearly dropped my phone. A Vegas gig was huge. Like monumental. Never in a million years had I expected to be offered the main spot in a Vegas performance. I would be an absolute idiot if I turned down something like this. But for some reason, the excitement was tinged with tendrils of anxiety. Could I really just leave like that? This should be any performer's dream. But suddenly it didn't feel like mine. It felt like it was actually taking me in the opposite direction of what I currently wanted.

"Dani?" Katie asked, concern lacing her tone.

"Yes. Sorry, I'm just honestly in a state of shock. This is

huge." My voice was breathy and foreign to my ears. Could she tell that my fight or flight response had kicked in?

Deep breaths, Dani. This was just a phone conversation.

"Don't be. Dani, you're an amazing performer. I'm not going to lie, I wasn't that upset when the other performer dropped out, because from the moment I took over the show from the previous director, I knew this role was for you," she said sweetly, and that in itself was a huge compliment. Again, it should have been excitement coursing through my veins, not anxiety.

"That's very nice of you to say, Katie," I said. Her words seemed to sink into my bones. This was the kind of validation an artist yearned for. I couldn't back away from this. The people-pleaser in me felt inclined to take this immediately. No one in their right mind would turn down something like this.

Okay. So, I needed to take this gig even if it wasn't what I really wanted. I needed to figure out how to make it work even if I was scared to lose Myla in the process. The show was temporary, and we could probably figure it out. We cared deeply about one another, and strong relationships spanned time and space if they were really meant to be. Long distance could be done easily, right? If anyone could make it work, it could be us. We had already overcome plenty, this would just be the next obstacle we took on together.

"So what do you say, Dani?" Katie asked, probably expecting only one answer.

"Er..." I cleared my throat. "Oh my god. Wow. Uh yes. I mean, yes, I want to be in your show. Don't you want to see a video or audition or something?" I asked. My emotions were swirling in an angry vortex in my stomach, and nausea rolled through me.

"Sure, but I trust you, and I know this is something you can handle. You are the only person this role was made for, and if you can't do it, we might change the show, honestly. But it would be for a whole month, so that's the run time of the show, and the pay is..." Katie said the number, and I gasped.

My phone nearly dropped out of my hand.

"You're saying you'll pay 150,000 dollars to come do this show?" I asked, not sure if I'd heard that right.

"It will be hard work. It's two shows a night, Wednesday through Sunday, for four weeks, but we need someone who can learn the choreo ASAP. We'll fly you out in a few days, because the show headlines in two weeks," Katie explained.

"Shit. Can you give me the day to wrap my head around this, and I'll get back to you?" I needed a second to breathe and figure out logistics. To tell Myla and figure out how I could have my cake and eat it too. With money like that on the line, there was no other answer besides *yes,* unfortunately.

"Of course. You're an incredibly talented performer, Dani. This show is huge. Tickets go for hundreds of dollars, and thousands for the VIP suites. Shoot me a text or give me a call when you're ready to commit." And then she hung up.

It felt like I was detached from real life, like that call hadn't even happened. Katie sent a text saying to not keep her waiting too long with a winky face. That was all I needed to send me plummeting back to earth and to know this opportunity was a once-in-a-lifetime experience that could open up doors I didn't even know existed. Is that what I wanted? I couldn't be sure anymore.

I walked back to Myla, feeling like my whole world just got flipped upside down and turned inside out.

"What happened? You look good? Bad? Honestly, I can't tell." Myla scanned my body, worry etching her brow.

"I just got offered a job for a Vegas gig. Four weeks, ten shows a week, for 150,000 dollars." Saying it out loud made it feel real and tangible. I nearly choked on the words coming out of my mouth.

"Holy shit!" Myla jumped up and gave me a hug. "That's

unheard of! You have to take it." Her touch seemed to ground me, and I wanted to sink into her warm embrace.

I swallowed. "But I will leave in the next few days and be gone for six weeks. Myla, I don't want to leave you and Cirque Callisto." The words were true, but it was also true I wanted that money, so I would need to do the show. Both things coexisted at the same time. It didn't make a damn bit of sense, though, because financially and career-wise, this was a no brainer. Why did I feel like I was oddly betraying the buds of our relationship? That was silly. Nothing would change. Six weeks was no big deal.

"We will be here when you get back, Dani. That is life-changing money and a life-changing opportunity," she whispered, and I nodded. It was. I could finally pay back my brother, or at least say thank you, and pay off my student loans. That was completely wild to think about. Soaren wouldn't want to accept the money, but I could at least spoil him and Lily some, just like they had spoiled me.

"I'll miss out on Brownie and Biscuit time." Why was I trying this hard to find reasons not to go instead of reasons to go? None of this made sense, and anxiety clawed its way up my throat and pricked the backs of my eyes. This was a million-in-one chance that could skyrocket my international career. Isn't that what I should want?

I had always drifted from place to place looking for the next adventure, but suddenly I found myself yearning to stay and grow here. To grow deep roots with someone I really cared about.

Was that naive or too idealistic?

I really had no idea.

"Again, we'll be right here. Let's talk about this more at home. I feel like maybe you need a moment to process. Lots of big things are happening today, and we can only do one thing at a time." Myla squeezed my hand, and the steadiness of her palm seemed to ground me a little more.

"Yes, okay. Let's focus on the little ones right now and talk about this later," I said.

"Celebrate this later," Myla corrected, giving me a peck on the cheek. "This is huge. Regardless of whatever happens, it is amazing you were offered this opportunity, Dani. You should be really proud of that." Tears were welling in her eyes, and she swiped at them.

Myla crying for me because she was truly proud of me was definitely in my top-ten favorite moments.

"Here they are!" The woman walked in with two carriers, one housing our little puppy and the other one holding our kitten.

"Thank you." Myla beamed as she reached for them.

"Call if you need anything." She handed us a folder, and we walked out.

We nodded and cooed at the little ones, who seemed nervous about taking a journey in the car, but I got them settled. The conversation with Katie sat heavy in my head.

The rest of the evening consisted of showing the two little ones around the house. They were shy and sleepy, barely walking out of the carriers, except to snuggle against one another, before they settled back into Biscuit's crate. We littered the ground around them with toys and treats, setting up spaces for them to snuggle and rest.

They barely lasted an hour before they were totally tuckered out, and the conversation that had been on repeat in my head needed to be said out loud.

"Dani, I can practically hear the wheels turning in your head. Tell me why this opportunity feels scary for you." She sat down next to me on the couch and tucked her legs underneath her.

"I'm afraid to break what we've built here. I know that

may seem silly and irrational, but it's making this opportunity feel confusing for me," I said truthfully. There was more to it, but I didn't have words for all the things going on in my chest right now.

"Okay, what else?" Myla asked, stroking my arm.

"This feels delicate between us. I don't want this to feel like I am abandoning you when we just disclosed our feelings for one another. We have been making plans to build something, like me being a part of the little fur babies' lives and yours... It's hard to feel like I won't do irreparable harm by leaving and forcing us to try long distance when we have had such little time together in the first place."

"I don't want your fears for us to be the reason you don't take this job. The little ones and I will be here when you get back. There's no pressure for you to keep our entire relationship together. It's a team effort, and even though it's okay to be scared, know that I have you. I want to support you and your dreams," Myla said, grabbing my hand and giving my knuckles a kiss, before settling our entwined fingers into her lap.

"Are you sure? I am not sure that this is my dream, but I would like to give it a shot." I looked at our hands together and desperately wanted to see this opportunity through and have Myla at the same time.

"Yes, no matter what happens, I'll be here for you." She straddled my lap and leveled her gaze to mine. I nodded and took a deep breath.

"Okay, I'll take the job." I smiled, and Myla squealed, sealing the deal with a kiss. Everything would be fine. Myla seemed sure of it, and she spent the rest of night showing me how sure of everything she was.

TWENTY-THREE
MYLA

I stared at the fabric while everyone else around me trained and chatted. My brain was a million miles away from this warehouse, and my body felt unlike my own. Every drill and trick felt heavy. Dani leaving was like a ticking time bomb, like my body was braced for impact. I knew we could handle it, but I was scared, too. There were a lot of conflicting emotions. Pride and excitement for this to fall into their lap, and fear they would love it there and never come back. This was an amazing opportunity, and there was no way Dani could pass it up. However, the thought of them leaving when we were just finding our rhythm felt daunting. Six weeks was nothing, right? My uneasiness was spiraling at everything that could happen in six long weeks.

Those weeks could be everything or nothing. How would we know until it was already happening? The feelings mixed together and formed a hard ball in my throat.

Brownie and Biscuit were just starting to settle in, and the thought of our little family being broken up was a sucker punch to the gut, even though I knew it was a no-brainer decision. This was temporary. The animals would be fine. I would be fine. Why couldn't I just shove these feelings away and be excited?

Ugh. When you loved someone, you wanted to hold them close and be with them twenty-four seven. Dani and I were just now exploring what that meant. But things would be okay. Other couples had done harder shit. This wouldn't change anything except put a minor six-week pause on things or make us grow fonder through distance. Surely it would make us appreciate one another and not shove us apart? There was no need to dive headfirst into worst-case scenarios.

My apprehension was about it happening this early. Things felt delicate; my life had just found its balance again.

"What's with the sad-girl look?" Logan asked, plopping down next to me, a little breathless from running a few things on the trapeze. She blew a long, pink strand of hair away from her eyes as she scanned my expression.

"It's permeating through the entire warehouse," Aven teased as she practiced a backbend on the floor. Frowning, I shot her a glare. Was it really that obvious I was losing my mind in the hamster wheel of emotions circling in my brain?

"Myla, what's wrong?" Jess asked, raising her brow. She joined me and Logan on the ground. Aven came out of her bridge and completed our little circle by sitting across from me. Maybe this was how Aven felt the other day when we all got on her about Bex. Suddenly I felt a little cornered, and my first instinct was to push them away and assure my friends that things were okay.

But that would be a lie. I wasn't okay, and talking would help. So, I hugged my knees closer to my chest and sighed.

"Fabric got you down? God knows it brings me down," Logan grumbled, and I sneered. She hated silks. They were never where she wanted them to be, but for me, it was fluid and moved under my command. It helped me stay in my own power even though I knew it felt the opposite for her. How funny that the same thing could be something so different to each of us.

"Dani was offered a job," I blurted out after all sets of their eyes burned into my skin for what felt like minutes, but was really seconds.

"Okay." Jess looked at me expectantly, waiting for the rest of the story.

"It's in Vegas. A huge job, with all the Vegas money. And they have to take it. It would be a game changer for their career and for their finances, but they would be gone over a month, and it makes me sad," I said as tears slid down my cheeks. Aven wrapped an arm around me, and I fell into her touch. It felt childish and irrational. I had no right to be this upset and taint Dani's success, but here I was wanting to sob at the thought of being without them for a measly month.

"That sucks for you all. Amazing opportunity for Dani, but sucks for your relationship nonetheless. Both things can happen at the same time, Myla. It's okay to feel excitement and sorrow. It's perfectly normal." Jess reached out and squeezed my leg.

"It can be scary to start a new relationship and then for something like this to happen. It's tough," Logan validated.

"And I know we can make it work. Like, logically, I understand that, but my heart hurts at the idea of them being gone for a long period of time." I sobbed into my hands, and it felt like my whole body ached.

Why did this feel like an arrow to my chest? They would be back. It didn't mean we were breaking up; it just meant we would be without one another for a minute.

"Why do you think it hurts this bad?" Logan nudged my knee with hers.

"Because..." I sniffled, trying to work through the ball of emotion stuck in my chest.

"Because what, Myla?" Logan asked gently.

"Because I love them." I had barely admitted it to myself, let alone to them or out loud. Our relationship felt safe and grounded in a way I hadn't ever experienced before, especially not in my many years with Jake. I wanted to protect that feeling and squirrel it away so the world couldn't taint or touch it.

Logan reached over and grabbed my hand, holding on tight.

"And we just started our little family together with pets and everything. I don't want that to go away. I feel like, for the first time in years, this is who I am supposed to be with and who I am supposed to love." I wiped snot from my face, and the tears continued to spill. I was terrified to be alone in that house again without their warmth and spirit. If I was being honest, I was terrified to do life without them in any capacity. My whole body yearned for their touch, their music, and their kindness. Never in my life had I felt this connected to someone else. Realizing that now, days before they were leaving, stole my breath away and made my bones dissolve into Jell-O.

"Myla, have you told them how you feel?" Jess gave me an encouraging smile.

"Not yet. We just found out about the job while we were getting the little ones, so we haven't had a chance to discuss it much." Everything was happening too fast. One thing after another, in a pile stacked too high. My insecurities soared, and I was terrified I would be buried under the weight of it all.

"I think you should lead with your heart. Six weeks feels like a lot right now, but you can make it work. I know they care about you deeply as well." Logan released my hand and hugged her own knees to her chest, resting her chin there.

"Relationships are hard," I muttered, leaning further into Aven's embrace.

"I mean, why do you think I'm on a hiatus?" Aven giggled next to me, and it made me laugh too.

"You say that, but you're still flirting around the edges with Bex," Jess threw at her.

"Hey, we're not here to talk about what may or may not be happening in my bed," Aven mumbled, putting up her walls again. How long would she resist before she let us and Bex in fully? She was tenacious, I would give her that.

"Why not? I would rather hear about that then talk about this right now. I know I need to talk to Dani, but I'm struggling to be vulnerable right now after everything with Jake. Distract me please," I begged, looking up at her, and she sighed.

"There isn't much to tell," Aven said in a quiet voice.

"Liar!" Logan accused.

"You know nothing!" she hissed playfully.

"Ah, well, you know, I have a sixth sense for these things. You all have hooked up at least a few times now, including after the drag show. And may still be regularly hooking up to this day?" Logan raised a brow at her, and Aven avoided her gaze.

"Anyway, how are you and Ozzie?" Aven looked at Jess, who laughed.

"Nice change. We're great. Nothing wild to report here. How's dating going for you, Logan?" she shot back as Logan was mid-drink, and she nearly spit her water out. The conversation was volleying back and forth to see who would spill their own gossip first.

"This conversation always seems to go around in circles," I muttered, considering we all had just been gabbing about this not long ago. No one wanted to budge, but here we were, needling one another anyway.

"You know, I have some things to do, so I'm exiting out of this tired old conversation. Myla, if you need me, I will be on the trapeze. The rest of you..." She looked at Aven and Jess, then flipped them off.

They roared with laughter as she sauntered away.

"The love bug comes when you least expect it," Jess said and got up to head back to her apparatus.

"You sure you'll be okay, Myla? I know there are a lot of conflicting emotions happening right now, and that's okay. You don't have to figure it all out on your own. We're here for you whenever you need us." Aven gave me a full squeeze, and I sunk into her embrace. Oh how I wished Aven would take her own advice.

"I know. This stuff is just hard. Especially after Jake, I just... feel guarded and scared for what distance could do to us. I mean, Jake was right here and I let the distance get too vast. What if I let that happen to me and Dani and we're too far away from one another, or I'm too late?" I tugged on my hair and tried to calm my racing heart.

"Hey, Myla." Aven turned to face me, grabbing my hand away from my hair.

"What?"

"The first step to being better is awareness. And this relationship is different. You know that, right?" She gently held my palm in hers, and the urge to tug or pick at my hair was strong, but her grip was stronger.

"I know it's different." I sighed, looking at our hands together.

"Dani wants to be with you. Just talk to them. Okay?" Aven stood up and dragged me to my feet.

"Thanks, Ave." I wrapped my arms around her and held on for a few moments.

"I'm going to go back to training, but we're all here if you need anything." She let me go and walked over to the acro mat.

"I'm going to go home and check on the babies." I gathered my things and headed out toward my house, unsure if Dani would be there or not. Biscuit and Brownie greeted me right away and demanded attention. I gave them scratches and kisses that soon turned into them wrestling one another as they rolled away.

My conversation with my friends kept playing in my head. The tears were at bay, but not for long. They wanted to pour out, but I was tired of crying today. I wanted to just enjoy the moment with the little ones before handling what was to come.

"Hey," Dani said from the kitchen, and my voice got caught in my throat. I was so lost in my own thoughts that I hadn't realized they were right there the whole time.

They were extraordinary. I didn't know how I was going to be okay without them for the next few weeks. Would they want to do long distance? Would they want to talk every day, or would that be too much?

I didn't know.

"Myla," Dani said, raising a brow, as if they could hear the inner dialogue firing aggressively in my brain.

I swallowed and made my way over to them. Going in for a hug, their warm touch grounded me. Wetness found its way back to my cheeks as I sobbed against their chest.

"I know. It's going to be okay," they soothed as we rocked slightly, and the little ones danced around our toes.

There was so much I wanted to say and express, but it all jumbled up, like a ball of yarn that needed to be unraveled, and I had no clue where to start or where to pull.

"I'm sorry, I'm getting you all wet," I said as I continued to snot and cry into their shirt.

"It's okay. Just let it out, and then we can talk about it, okay?"

At some point, we moved to the couch, and the tears stopped, but I stayed glued to their side, unable to let go or say anything that would make myself feel better.

So I stayed like that for as long as I could, and eventually I fell asleep, wishing the words I wanted to say would flow easily and they would return the sentiment.

TWENTY-FOUR
DANI

I woke up and saw Myla's sleeping form next to me. The worry in her brows and mouth had been erased by sleep. The two little ones were snuggled at our feet, purring and snoring softly.

Her emotions had been hard to navigate yesterday. I didn't know how much me moving would really affect her. It made me nervous about leaving her. Would she be okay? Would we be okay? She seemed to be putting on a front for me. I knew this would be harder than she let on, but I didn't know how much. Would the strain be too much? What would happen if she wanted to end it while I was gone?

Taking deep breaths, I tried to calm my rampant thoughts. It was normal to be intimidated by such a big transition. It didn't mean everything we'd built would come toppling down; it would just be put on pause.

Even though I knew all those things logically, there was still a little gremlin in my brain poking at my negative thoughts and making my panic blossom.

Part of me thought the money wasn't worth it. The

emotional part of me wanted to say screw it and stay here, taking care of Myla and the babies. However, the logical part of me knew that wasn't possible. If we were meant to be, we would get through it. There was really no question in my decision, except the niggling, intrusive thoughts were rampant. The more I settled into leaving, the more my brain told me it would rip this relationship apart.

These thoughts are not facts, Dani.

Catastrophizing the situation would not help, so I tried to shove out all the drama my head was keen on bringing up. I knew they weren't true, but I couldn't help but listen to the hollering in my mind every once in a while. They seemed determined to steal my attention.

This show would catapult my finances and my performance career. I would have an abundance of options with this gig. I could literally retire early if I played my cards right. Not that I wanted that, but this cracked my circus world wide open. But is that what I wanted now? Moving from place to place used to be fun and exciting, but then, once I landed with Soaren and Lily, I started to yearn for a home that was mine. I guess inadvertently the things I wanted had changed, and I hadn't taken much time to explore what that actually meant.

Would it be totally ridiculous to say this Vegas show was actually not what I dreamed of anymore? The intensity and stress of a show this big for the next month was doable, but after that? The idea of doing this forever and ever made my body feel heavy in a way I couldn't explain. My nervous system had a hard time comprehending this type of show, day in and day out. Yes, I would be stable with money, but what about my mental and physical health? It was too late now. I couldn't rescind my acceptance.

And I knew Myla would never let me turn this down either. She would do whatever she needed to do to push me to go. We could do long distance for a little over a month, if that's what she wanted to do. I could easily commit to that, and then we could see where things were after that.

One day at a time was all we could do right now, and it would have to be good enough.

Myla groaned, and her purple hair moved to fall into her eyes. I carefully brushed it away and ran my fingertips along her cheeks.

"Dani," she mumbled.

"Yes?" I whispered.

"Are you watching me sleep?" She pried open one eye and smiled goofily. It was easy to get lost in the depth of her brown eyes as they scanned my face.

"You're impossible not to look at, Myla. Of course, I'm watching you sleep." I brushed my lips across her forehead. My body hummed next to her, in tune to every breath and flutter of her eyelashes.

"Sorry I cried all over you last night with little to no explanation." She opened her other eye, and shame clouded her features. Oh how I wished I could wash that feeling away. Her feelings were meant to be felt, and if they happened to be felt all over me, then I wasn't complaining too much. When you cared for someone, you wanted to hold them through it all, the good and the bad.

"You don't need to be sorry, Myla. Your feelings are valid. Big things are happening right now, and I would love to talk about it. But I understand the need for an emotional release. You can cry as much as you need with me. You don't need to hide your heart from me," I said, stroking her hair and wishing I could press pause right here with her body next to mine.

Myla sat up and looked at me with a serious expression.

"I don't want to break up." She started tugging at her hair, then bit her lip. My shoulders relaxed just a little at that.

"I don't either," I responded.

"So, can we do long distance until you come back?" she asked, casting her eyes down, as if the answer would be anything but a resounding yes.

I grabbed her chin and forced her to look back at me. "Of course. I would love nothing more. This will just be a new adventure to face together." God, I wanted to believe the words coming out of my mouth. The cool confidence I was trying to exude was the opposite of what my wildly beating heart was feeling.

"It petrifies me," she whispered, her lip trembling. Her emotional state was fragile. Myla had just left a long-term relationship because her partner couldn't show up for her, and now I was leaving. I was sure this fed into her own relational baggage. I hated that this paralleled her previous situation, but we were different. Our relationship was nothing like what she'd had before, and I was determined to keep it that way.

"I know. But we can do it together. I'll be sad to miss these weeks with you and our little ones." I looked at the little furballs fondly. They were still passed out, making small noises as they dreamed.

"But we can do it, right?" Myla pleaded with her features.

"Of course we can. We can do anything," I promised her, and I hoped it was true. Some of the tension seemed to ease from the room with that declaration. "I have an idea for what we should do today."

"And what's that?" she asked, the brightness in her eyes coming back.

"Let's make a fort and order takeout and stay in with one another today. A celebratory last date before things get wild and I have to leave. What do you say?" I asked, wanting to just bask in her presence a little longer before I would be gone.

"I've never made a fort before!" Myla squealed. Biscuit and

Brownie began to stir, then made their way up the bed for pats and kisses.

We each grabbed a furball and cooed at them.

"Okay, I'll get to feeding them, and you start to think of what snacks and food you want today so we only have to leave the house once." I wished I could just pause time for a moment and savor each second here.

Myla saluted me, and I got to work getting breakfast for Biscuit and Brownie.

Myla texted me a list, and I quickly went to the store and grabbed some food along the way back. Myla was still in her pajamas when I arrived back at the house, which was perfect for our stay-at-home date.

"I got all the goods," I said, holding up the bags of food and treats.

"Wooo!" Myla cheered as she sat on the floor playing with the two little ones.

Quickly, I put everything away and sat down with her, joining in on the fun as they tumbled over one another and made little growls and grumbles.

"Are you ready for this fort?" I lifted my brows as Myla's eyes glittered.

"Heck yeah I am!"

We slowly grabbed blankets, pillows, and other miscellaneous items to make our masterpiece. We draped fabric over the couch and used some chairs as peaks for the fort. We ended up making a tunnel and a little alcove where we dragged a laptop in to watch something.

It felt magical and all our own.

"I like this life we're creating together." Myla stroked Biscuit's fur, then scratched Brownie's ears.

"Me too."

"Before you leave, I have a request." Myla avoided my eyes

and cleared her throat. I sat up straighter, ready for whatever she threw at me.

"I want to reclaim my bed." Her eyes met mine then, and there was a fire there that made my heart flutter.

"Tell me more." I squeezed her knee, and her tongue wet her lips.

"I want it to have memories of us, not Jake and me. I'm tired of avoiding it and being afraid to go in there. It's my bed, and I want to make it known that it is." Her confidence seemed to be growing as she told me what she wanted.

"What would you like to do on this bed?" I murmured, leaning in closer, our noses were almost touching.

"Probably some of this." Myla reached up and cupped my jaw, letting her lips lightly touch mine before slowly diving deeper. Her tongue slid against mine, and her other hand snaked into my hair.

The kiss was slow and sensual, making my toes curl as we explored one another's mouths and ran our fingertips along each other's skin.

"And what else, Myla?" I asked in a breathy tone.

"Definitely some of this." Myla was all bravado now as she pushed me down against our mound of pillows and started running her mouth along my collarbones, and across my hips and inner thighs. I arched into her as her mouth and fingertips played closer to my hot center.

Suddenly the two little ones decided they wanted to be involved, and they pounced on my face with aggressive little licks and nips. We both burst out laughing as I tried to manage the little attack on my skin.

"Okay, okay, you two! Maybe we will try defacing my bed later?" Myla gently grabbed them away from my face.

Wiping tears from my eyes, I sat up. "That will for sure not be the last time that happens."

"I know. They will most definitely feel left out if they

don't get to be involved." Myla popped some popcorn in her mouth and smiled lovingly at the two of them as they tumbled around in the fort together.

I cleared my throat. "I know that me leaving is more complicated due to the nature of you and Jake. I just want you to know I see you." I grabbed Myla's hand and stroked her knuckles, loving the feel of our skin together.

"Part of me feels like I'm losing my mind over nothing, you know? A month or so is not that long. The other part of me is whispering in my ear of what a dumbass I am to have started this with you in the first place. And the part I know to be true is that I care about you deeply, and you leaving is temporary," she said, her voice wobbling.

"I know." I didn't have the right words to say. I pressed a kiss to her temple instead.

"I bet Logan will be thrilled to come over and do auntie duties on B&B," Myla joked.

"Yes, I'm sure."

"I wonder if Bex and Aven will get their stuff figured out," Myla said, intertwining our fingers together.

"I think they will, but it might take some time." Those two were just setting themselves up for something messy, but Bex seemed to like it and Aven seemed to be avoiding it. He was committed, though, I would give him that.

"That just leaves Logan as the last single person left," Myla said, tapping her fingers against her thigh.

"I think she likes being alone, though. She wouldn't settle for anything less than perfect, you know. I can't wait to get your updates when I'm gone," I said, stroking the soft skin along Myla's arms. I loved the way little goosebumps popped up anywhere we touched.

The rest of the evening, we tried to enjoy one another's company, letting the thought of me leaving take a back seat to being with one another and playing with the little ones.

I had to keep reminding myself that, even though I was leaving, I had a home to come back to, which felt better than I could have even imagined. Cirque Callisto and Myla were where my heart was, and I would be damned if I didn't protect that with all I had.

Twenty-Five
Myla

"Dani," I breathed, twining our fingertips together.

"Myla?" they asked, a mischievous glint in their eyes.

This was the night I would take back what was rightfully mine. No longer would my bed have power over me. Even though, if I was being honest with myself, I still would prefer to sleep in Dani's bed, just because it was theirs.

But I wanted to stake a new claim on that stupid mattress. Dani was leaving soon, and I needed to face my demons and show that bed who was boss.

"Let's have sex in my bed tonight."

"Are you sure?" they asked, even though I was already walking us toward my room. The little ones were tuckered out from our evening together, and there would be no interruptions to the things I wanted to do to Dani's body and what I wanted them to do to mine.

"God yes. Please can I make you come on that haunted mattress?" I pleaded, dragging them into my room and shutting the door behind me.

"Myla, I would love to make you scream on these sheets so

anytime you look at this bed, all you can think of is how your pussy is mine," they whispered, crowding me into the door. I shivered as their words licked against my skin. Immediately I was wet, and I wanted nothing more than for our naked bodies to be right against one another.

"Jesus, Dani," I said as they kissed along my jawline and feathered their fingertips up my arms.

"Take your clothes off, Myla," Dani commanded, their eyes hungry as they scanned my face. They watched as I slowly and deliberately slipped my tank top off, then slid out of my shorts.

"Now you," I said, wanting to see their body as desperately as they devoured mine with their gaze.

"Let me just look at you," they purred as they took a perusal from head to toe, stopping to lick their lips when their gaze landed on my tits, then the small patch of hair at the apex of my thighs. Wetness slid against my inner thighs as heat licked up my spine.

"You're breathtaking, Myla. Absolutely stunning." My heart nearly exploded at the compliment. Our eyes connected and, without saying anything, Dani slipped off their own clothes.

They were magnificent. All muscular lines with the tiny bars of silver through their nipples. My mouth watered thinking about taking their piercings inside my mouth and watching them fall apart underneath my touch.

I could taste the memory of their pleasure ingrained in my mouth. Was it possible to get even wetter just from looking at them?

"Eyes up here, Myla," Dani teased as I licked my lips and snapped my gaze to them.

"Kiss me, please," I begged, and they didn't need another reminder. They caged me in against the door, and their lips found mine like we were made for one another. I groaned into them as they nipped at my bottom lip and their tongue explored the inside of my mouth.

"Dani," I groaned, sliding my hands into their fiery red hair and scraping against their scalp as they pressed their body into mine. We felt like two perfect puzzle pieces fitting together, all naked flesh and delicious pleasure.

In a team effort, we walked over to the bed and, feeling bold, I shoved Dani hard so they landed on the white sheets. Laughing, they propped up on their elbows as I slid down on the ground in between their legs.

"You look good between my knees, Myla."

I preened at the praise as I kissed up their strong thighs and dug into their hip bones with my fingers. I made my way up to their wet center and took a long swipe against their cunt with my tongue. They quaked underneath me.

Sliding my hands underneath their ass, I found their clit and began circling with my tongue as I gently slid one and then two fingers into their wet folds.

"That's it, Myla." Dani's hips ground against my face as I sucked and licked their essence, wanting them to come all over my face. My arousal was soaking my legs, but I wouldn't stop until Dani came first. I wanted them to cry out and feel, with every swipe of my tongue, how much I wanted them and what they did to me.

Dani's legs began to shake, and I stayed constant in my pressure as they clenched around me and moaned my name. I licked them through their ecstasy until the clenching of their inner walls relaxed, and they gently pulled on my hair to pull me up.

"You look positively lovely with my cum all over your face," they mused as I kissed and licked my way back up their body, giving special attention to their piercings as they arched off the bed.

Dani grabbed my chin and hauled me up, tasting themself

on my lips. Our limbs entangled, their thighs sliding against my clit and their hands massaging my ass.

"I need to taste you. Straddle my face," Dani commanded, and my mouth opened in a little *o*.

"Are you sure I won't, like, crush you?" I asked, suddenly self-conscious.

"Darling, if I drowned in you, it would be my favorite way to go," they teased, and I giggled as they grabbed at my hips and tried to move me up. We wiggled up the bed so my hands were placed on the wooden headboard and I was hovering above their grinning face.

"Like this?" I asked. They nodded and grabbed my hips, pulling me down and spearing me on their tongue. I cried out and let my weight settle as their skilled tongue went to work on my clit. I moaned as I ground against them, and they ate me out like it was their fucking job.

A wave of pleasure was building inside me with every swipe of their tongue, and I moved faster, needing more friction.

"Dani, I'm close," I said as I continued to rock against them. Their fingertips were gripping my ass, and I pulled at my nipples. Suddenly I was falling over the edge, and I cried out as Dani continued to lick me through my release. My thighs were probably crushing their skull, but I couldn't stop the way my body was quaking around them. I nearly collapsed to the side of them, breathing heavily. Dani pulled me in and kissed my lips gently.

The taste of me on their lips did something primal to me. It made me want to crawl into their embrace and never leave.

"Dani," I breathed. I didn't even know what I was trying to say, but I wanted them to know they meant the world to me. There were too many words stuck in my throat that I didn't know how to get out.

"I know, Myla," they whispered against my skin, and

maybe they did. We both seemed too afraid to utter all the words left unsaid so soon before they were leaving. It felt too much like a goodbye, but also too much like a promise neither one of us knew we could keep.

"Thank you for defiling this bed with me." I giggled, realizing this silly piece of furniture no longer had power over me.

"I would happily fuck you on any piece of furniture," they teased, and we wrapped ourselves around one another.

"I will probably still sleep in your bed, though, while you're gone. Then when you come back, maybe I could just stay there for, you know, an indefinite amount of time..." I trailed off, letting this be a sad excuse for the commitment I couldn't actually get out of my mouth.

"My bed is yours," Dani whispered, and I nodded as our lips found one another again. We spent the rest of the night showing this damn bed who was boss.

————

The days leading up to Dani's departure went by too fast. There was a heaviness that continued to pull at my heart that I struggled to articulate. I wanted to enjoy our time together before they left, but my ability to be present was deeply affected by my anxiety.

We did our best to be there for one another as we bonded more deeply with Brownie and Biscuit. Our little family seemed to be knitting itself closer together until the very moment Dani was packing up their bags.

I sat on their bed as they packed for the weeks ahead. The little ones passed out on the comforter, curled into one another. I stroked their fur, the presence of them calming me. Dani was going back and forth between the bathroom and their room, grabbing what they needed for the journey ahead.

"How are you feeling about the show?" I pulled at my hair

as Dani folded and stashed clothes in their luggage. We were set to go to the airport in just a few hours.

"Good. Kind of nervous, because I don't exactly know what I'm walking into. Will I be able to do the role how they imagined it, or will they have to inevitably change their vision because of my skills?" Dani furrowed their brow and fidgeted with the clothes.

"Dani, they know what kind of performer you are. There will ultimately be things that need to be changed to accommodate who you are versus who the other performer was, but that's normal," I said, placing my palm in theirs, and they stared at our hands stacked one on top of the other.

"I know."

"Plus, they reached out to you. They pursued you. They want you," I reassured them, squeezed their fingertips.

"I think I'm worried I might disappoint them." Dani swallowed and looked up to meet my eyes.

"You won't." I knew in my heart Dani would be amazing.

"I'm also worried I'll disappoint you," they whispered. I scooted off the bed to wrap my arms around their muscular shoulders.

"You won't." I squeezed them tight and placed a kiss on their forehead. "Your worry just means you care deeply, and that's one of the many, many things I absolutely love about you." Dani's eyes scanned my face, and they placed a light kiss to my lips before resting their forehead against mine.

In my heart, the words *I love you* were already branded inside me when it came to Dani. But I didn't want to do this right before they left. What if they didn't say it back, and I messed up this already difficult situation?

"Thank you, Myla." Dani's breath whispered across my cheeks, and my heart squeezed with the desire to get my feelings fully out in the open. But I held back, not wanting to move too fast, too soon. To overwhelm our emotional plates.

"Let's get you packed up and off to the airport." I pulled away and smiled, trying to make it as genuine as possible despite my heart ripping in two with this much left unsaid.

"Right." Dani cleared their throat and went back to grabbing all their things. We still needed to swing by the studio to grab some of the equipment they would need for their trip.

Thirty minutes later, the little ones were put away in their crates and we headed out. We pulled up, and everyone cheered when we walked in.

"Congrats, Dani!" Logan blew into one of those cheap noisemakers while Jess twirled around another thing that sang. Ozzie and Bex popped little confetti poppers.

"We are incredibly proud of you!" Bex beamed at them, and Dani's face melted into a megawatt smile.

"You all are too sweet. I didn't know you would be here." Dani's eyes sparkled.

"Oh my god, if you cry, we're all going to cry," Aven said, coming forward to grab Dani for a hug.

"I'm just really thankful for you all and this community. Having a place to call home is new to me, and even though it's just for a little over a month, I will miss you all deeply." Dani went around and hugged everyone as I gathered their things.

"How are you holding up, Myla?" Logan snuggled up next to me.

"Uh, I'm fine." My voice came out scratchy, and my stomach felt funny.

"Myla." Aven came up next to me and raised her brow.

"We can talk about it later, okay? I'm coming back after I drop them off, so I'll be back in a little bit."

I rushed around, trying to avoid everyone's inquiries about my feelings and keep things focused on Dani and their accomplishments. It was a short-lived get-together, as Dani's flight was looming ahead. More hugs were exchanged and promises to see one another soon.

Slipping my hand into Dani's, we scooted out and double-checked they had everything they needed.

"You did that, didn't you?" Dani asked as I drove.

"I wanted you to feel loved and supported with this, and to know we aren't going anywhere." I flashed a smile as tears were running down their cheeks.

"That's the sweetest thing anyone has ever done for me. Thank you, Myla." They squeezed my knee, and I fought a blush on my cheeks.

"I know we've prepped this goodbye a million times, but I will miss you and I care about you a lot. I..." The words were right there, but I didn't want to do this in the car on the way to the airport... despite how much they fought to free themselves from my lips.

"I know. Me too," Dani said, interlacing their fingers in mine. The rest of the ride was in silence until we pulled up to the terminal. I got out and helped pull everything out, and then the moment was there. The one we had both been bolstering ourselves for, that really meant nothing and everything all at once.

"Okay, go kick some butt." I pulled on Dani's shirt and pressed myself to them, our lips and hands tangling with one another, to say all the things caught in my chest I couldn't get out.

"Okay, bye, Myla. I'll be back for you," they promised, and then turned and left. I watched them walk through the doors and tried to fight back a sob. They turned back and waved one last time. My chest felt flayed open, my heart sinking down into my stomach as I got back in my car and drove away.

They'd said they would text me when they got to their gate, when they took off, and then landed. I blasted the music, trying to drown out my thoughts and the waves of emotion rippling through me.

I drove straight back to the studio, where everyone was still chatting and playing with the noise toys, rehearsals seemingly forgotten. I stepped inside, and everyone's eyes looked at me. I burst into tears. They all rushed toward me, holding me together while my emotions poured out from every part of me.

It felt like I was letting go of Jake, the move, Dani coming in, our time together, all my feelings from them leaving, and everything else that had been heavy on my heart for the last few months.

Logan handed me a tissue, and I blew into it.

"Why don't we cancel rehearsal today and have some chill time?" Aven offered as my sobs turned into little hiccups.

"Logan's the boss," I said in a little whisper.

"Let's do it. We can make it up tomorrow. Nothing's pressing today, and we want to take care of you." Logan gave me a little squeeze.

"I say we get some yummy tacos and margaritas and drown our woes in tequila," Bex offered.

"I like this idea a lot," Ozzie mused as Jess began to close up the space.

"I'm in," I said, and we all clamored into our cars and headed to our favorite local spot.

"I have an idea that may or may not make you feel better," Logan said as we all settled up our drink and food orders.

"Okay," I said. My tears were dried for now, but I knew another wave would come when I was by myself at home with the little fur babies all alone. The thought of being a single parent to them gave me a new sense of overwhelm, but I pushed it down.

"Why don't we all plan to go to Vegas to see one of Dani's performances?" Logan smiled at us mischievously.

"Really? Can we squeeze that in with everything else? And how much does a flight to Vegas cost?" Aven asked, shock written across her face.

"Yeah. I've got a hookup in Vegas that can house us for free, and I've got loyalty points to use. My parents like to offer miles to me, and I would be happy to use them on you all," Logan said nonchalantly.

"Since when did you become our sugar mama?" Jess laughed, shaking her head.

"I mean, I'm down. We could just go for the performance, then come back. Surely a night off wouldn't hurt us!" Ozzie said excitedly.

"I like it. I like it a lot. Thank you, Lo." I loved my people and how they showed up for me.

"Then it's settled. I'll look at a few options and get back to you all about a date that works around our class and rehearsal schedules." She clapped her hands excitedly. Logan held up her glass for a toast, which we all wholeheartedly participated in.

I felt a little lighter knowing I would get to see Dani for just a little bit in between the long stretch of them being gone.

"So did you tell Dani you love them?" Bex asked casually, and I nearly spit out my drink.

"Bex!" Aven hollered, laughing.

"What?!" He blew a kiss at her, and her cheeks turned pink.

"How do you know that?" I asked, my mouth dropping open.

"I mean, I didn't know for sure until right now. But you do love them. Did you tell them?" Bex tilted his head to the side as Ozzie snickered.

"Okay, but now we do actually need to know." Jess blinked her eyes at me innocently, and I couldn't help but laugh.

"I didn't." I chewed my lip.

"Why not?" Ozzie asked gently.

"I didn't feel like it was the best time to say it right before they left. It felt like a lot to hurtle into one moment, you know?"

"I think every rom-com would beg to differ, but I see your point." Logan sipped her drink.

"And I'm afraid. What if they don't feel the same way, or it's too soon? Like I would have sent them off saying 'I love you' on this weird note of them not sure they could say it back? I don't know, it was too volatile for me to say it right before they left. Plus, if I still feel this way after they get back, I know that it's genuine and true." I took a bite of a chip in front of me, trying to give my rambling mouth something else to do.

"Love is scary," Bex said gently, his eyes fluttering to Aven, who pointedly looked away.

"Say it when you're ready. But either way, we're happy for you, Myla. I know this feels hard, but you're growing and healing with an amazing person. We're glad you found someone who cares for you the way you deserve." Jess's words warmed my heart, and I sighed.

"Okay, enough of this sad and sappy stuff. Someone else please tell me something else that is going on." I took a long drink, and Logan went into some story of some gigs coming up and funny requests she had gotten. Things would move fast while Dani was gone, and soon we would see them up on the big stage. Everything was working out just the way it was supposed to.

TWENTY-SIX

DANI

The shows were flying by, and now I was nearly halfway through. The cast and crew were amazing. Katie was phenomenal, and Vegas itself was a wild ride. But I knew in my heart that what I'd thought I wanted before wasn't what I wanted now. Myla and I hardly had time to chat besides quick texts and calls. I would get done tremendously late, and she often had to be up early for privates.

My chest hurt from missing her, and I seemed to choke on my words when we would talk on the phone, unable to articulate all I wanted to say about how I felt and what I wanted. What if she wasn't interested in the long haul? Nervousness crept in the longer we were apart. But I knew in my bones that, even though I loved this opportunity presented to me, it wasn't something I wanted to do constantly. I had found my community, and I wanted to get back to them.

The realization I didn't need to be a big-time performer, always on the road traveling and chasing the next best thing, hit me hard. There was a lot of pressure when you were an artist to be the best and find the big break. What they didn't tell you was it wasn't the only pathway. There were many ways to do the things you loved for a comfortable income. What I wanted was a community and stability... and to give my body a breather for a minute.

The thought settled into me with a comfort I didn't know I craved until now. I could make meaningful art and creative strides without it being on the biggest stage in the world. In some ways, it released some of the pressure I had put on myself when I'd begun this journey.

Performing at this rate was putting wear and tear on my body I no longer wanted. I would finish strong, but I needed a little less intensity, and what I really wanted was to be back with Myla, Biscuit, and Brownie. God, I missed some of the ease that went into being with the same core group of people who truly cared for your everyday life and not how much you could give on stage.

The people here cared, but they also put the show first and foremost. We were all here to do our job, and do it well. Everything else was less important.

I battled with how to talk to Myla about it. Should I wait until I got back? That seemed like an eternity too long, but I hated the idea of trying to do it on the phone. When was a good time to tell someone you wanted to hold on to your life together and do anything you could to love and protect it? And how could I tell her after us only really dating for a few weeks?

Even though we had lived and slept together for longer, it felt like maybe the intensity of my feelings might scare her. Where would we go from here? Would I still live with her? Would I move out?

I had no idea what the future would bring, but I knew I wanted to be back with my found family. Looking at my phone, I had the urge to call Myla and tell her, right now, how I felt. Instead, Soaren's name popped up, and my shoulders relaxed.

"Hey, Soaren." I lay down on my bed, double-checking the time, as I had to get to the event center in the next few hours to start warming up for tonight's show.

"Dani!" Soaren said, and then Lily echoed the cry as well.

"My favorite people!"

"How would you feel about me seeing your show?" Soaren asked casually, and I gasped.

"What? What about Lily? It's definitely an adult cabaret."

"I know, silly goose. I was thinking I would come out for the last weekend and have Lily stay with one of our friends."

"Daddy has to go see your show, and then tell me all about it, but, like, the kid version!" Lily said into the phone, and I laughed.

"I would love it. That would be amazing. You don't have to, but it would mean a lot to me." Tears welled in my eyes. My brother was truly the best, and I was grateful he would fly out to see me.

"This is huge, Dani, and I want to see you in Vegas," Soaren said happily.

"I don't know that I will ever be here to perform again, so this might be your only time to come see me," I teased.

"You'll be there again if you want, and if you don't, then I'll gladly follow your performances around." His voice was soft, and his words hit me right in the heart. Was he a mind reader, or did he just say that to be nice?

"I don't know that I want this anymore," I whispered. The words left my mouth before I could even think to stop them, and they felt heavy in the air around me.

"Want to talk about it?" Soaren asked patiently as Lily sang along to some songs in the background.

"I love performing, but the intensity of this is a lot. It feels more like a job and less like my specific artistry, you know? I love the feeling of being on stage, but it isn't a collaborative community. It's wonderful money and exposure, but it puts the show above the individual artists in so many ways despite the great management here..." The sentence trailed off even though there was more on my mind.

"And?" Soaren asked.

"And I miss my people. I miss my girl." Soaren knew I was seeing someone, but I hadn't said how serious things had gotten for me.

"Ah, Myla. Love is a powerful tool, and so is community. All the money in the world can't fill the void of those two things. It can help a lot of things, but unfortunately, those two things are one of a kind," he said gently.

"This sort of rigor is incredible for a short stint of time, but the Vegas life is not the life for me."

"Dani, I'm shocked!" he teased, and I laughed.

"Thanks for letting me talk it out. I'm excited to settle into the home I've created."

"Sometimes you have to leave somewhere to know that's where you're really meant to be."

I sighed loudly, letting some of the anxiety go on my exhale. "Okay, well that means I'll get to see you in just a few short weeks, and after that I'll go home. But right now, I've got to go eat and get ready," I said, standing up to get moving.

"Love you, Dani," Soaren said.

"Love you too, Soaren," I replied

"Lubbbbbb youuuuuu, Danioooo!" Lily hollered in the background.

"Bye, Lily! Love you!" I hung up and gathered my things. Ease worked its way into my bones, and my chest felt a little less tight. Saying what I wanted out loud, and to Soaren, made it feel a little less intense. I could tell Myla what was in my heart when I got back. I knew what I wanted, and I wanted to tell her.

Within the hour, I was in the dressing rooms, starting to put on my face and warming up when Katie came in. The other performers smiled and chatted around us. Katie did her best to care for everyone in the show and check in with all the performers to see if they needed anything, but she was just one person.

"Dani! Can I chat with you privately for a few moments?" She beamed at me.

"Of course." I followed her out of the dressing rooms and headed toward her office. "Everything okay?"

"It's fantastic! All the shows have been selling out, and everyone has just been raving about it. Especially you! The people love you, and some of the large donors are very interested in patroning your time and career here in Vegas." She slid her glasses back up the bridge of her nose.

"That is very kind. I don't even know what to say." I pulled at my ear, not knowing how to process this information.

"I debated on whether to tell you this before the show, but I like transparency and giving people all the information. There are several big-time donors here tonight who have already seen the show. They're VIPs, and they've brought along some of their investor friends. They're specifically enthralled with your performance on straps with your flute. If all goes well tonight, I'm expecting them to extend a huge show contract for you to be here for the next few years." Katie clapped her hands excitedly.

"Wow" was all that came out of my mouth, and Katie smiled at me knowingly.

"I know this is a lot of information, and you're probably a little shocked by it. You'll be amazing tonight. Don't let it make you nervous, okay? We'll talk after the show. I just thought you should know." She left quickly, and I shakily made my way back to the dressing rooms.

Did the money and fame matter that much to me? My insides twisted together. I felt confident in my decision before about the Vegas life not being for me, but what if I was offered something ridiculous?

I knew in my blood this wasn't for me, but maybe I should just get through it for the next year if offered something extraordinary? The thought oddly made me nauseous. But the idea of turning down a huge contract was unheard of. People would think I was stupid and naive.

But this just wasn't where I wanted to be. There was no guarantee I would be offered anything, anyway. I would just need to do my best tonight and deal with whatever happened afterward. I compartmentalized my feelings and tried to clear my head by warming up on the flute.

My phone was buzzing with "Merde" from everyone in the group, including Myla. She had sent me a picture of Brownie and Biscuit earlier with a message saying they missed me. That filled my heart with more joy than I could even put into words.

The clock ticked down until showtime as we all got into costume and final stage checks.

Tension was threaded through the air as Katie gave her final pep talk before the show, wishing us all good luck and telling us she was proud to work with us. She said all the right things. I should have been dying to stay here.

I shook my head and cleared my thoughts, and then the show began.

It was time to do my job.

Twenty-Seven

Myla

My knees bounced aggressively as the crowd hummed around us.

"This is amazing!" Aven commented while sipping her cocktail. We had made it to Dani's show, and everyone showed up Vegas-ready. We got in a few hours ago and went to work with glitter, rhinestones, and leather donning our little group. Logan had gotten us a hotel room right across from the event center, and it had been a whirlwind in the last twelve hours.

"Honestly kind of sad we aren't staying longer, but, you know, I think the gig tomorrow would be pretty pissed if we didn't show up." Logan sighed. It was all hands on deck tomorrow evening for an event, and even though Logan had offered to take me off it, I'd declined.

This was a surprise to Dani, and I didn't want to assume they would want me to stay longer, considering they didn't know we were here in the first place. I wanted it to be a surprise. We had barely exchanged more than a few minutes here and there over the phone and over text. I missed them with my whole freaking body. I just wanted to feel their skin and hear their laugh. It was like I was in withdrawal.

Both our schedules were chaotic right now. There wasn't a lot of time for us to truly sit down and chat. The last few weeks had been a blur as Brownie and Biscuit settled in and I became a single pet mom. It wasn't my favorite, but I was managing. I desperately wanted Dani to come back, though. Sleeping without them made me feel empty and sad, like a piece of my heart was missing, and the hole in my chest threatened to swallow me up if I didn't deal with it soon. The life we had been creating was something I deeply loved and yearned for. I hoped they felt the same way. Surely they did? We hadn't explicitly spelled out all our feelings, but I couldn't be the only one who was utterly smitten, right? Did this time away make their heart grow fonder, or were they glad to have been rid of me these last few weeks?

All these thoughts swirled around my brain like a tsunami, threatening to slam into me and knock me over.

"Last drink call, anyone?" Ozzie raised her brows and looked at us. I shook my head at her, and Jess got up and walked to grab one final cocktail.

"Vegas does have a special kind of allure. But god, just the idea of Dani's rehearsal schedule makes me exhausted," Bex commented, looking through the programs that had been handed out at the doors. It was a type of rigor that could easily crush you physically and spiritually. The stakes were high, and you were expected to perform no matter the cost. I knew their creative director was kind, but they still had a job to do. Just like Dani had been called in to replace their last lead, they wouldn't hesitate to kick someone off the stage if they weren't up to par.

"The intensity is killer. We have barely had time to chat. They mentioned it was hard on their body being here, but they were enjoying it." I tugged at my hair and wondered how they were actually doing. As a performer, it was easy to push through for the show, but then usually shit caught up with you afterward. We wanted to do our best and deliver on what we'd promised. This was our job, and Dani was getting paid a lot to be here, which added even more pressure to the situation.

We sacrificed unintentionally for our art, and our bodies ended up taking the brunt of it. Sometimes without us even really noticing it until it was too late.

"God, the post-show fatigue used to throw me on my ass," Logan muttered. "It was absolutely brutal. I wouldn't realize how bad it was until I let myself feel it, and then it was usually fucking debilitating."

We all nodded in agreement. The lights dimmed and the music changed as Jess and Ozzie slid back in at the last moment.

The crowd cheered as the lights went out, and a spotlight found a woman in the crowd who started to sing in a low, husky voice. The show was very much an adult love story with all the drama, skills, and theatrics you would expect at a Vegas show. Dani was one of the love interests. Jealousy slithered its way across my skin at the idea of them pretending to have feelings for someone else, and I mentally batted them away. This was our job. It was pretend. No need to get worked up over nothing. I didn't have much time to dwell on it, because my breath caught in my throat.

Dani flew across the stage on straps, their own strappy costume showing off their toned muscles and broad shoulders. They tangled themselves up and were pulled so high up toward the ceiling, I nearly gasped as they spun so aggressively everything probably blurred. They were a work of art in motion. Truly a sight to behold.

My eyes were glued to the stage as Dani did their straps solo, then was joined by the other love interest. That funny pang of jealousy erupted in my bones again as this stunning woman strutted around Dani. She was touching and dancing on them, making me see red.

Stop it, Myla, I mentally tried to scold myself.

They were both really freaking good at their jobs, because the tension in here was palpable as they moved and danced around one another. They moved to a partner acrobatics piece that was joined by other couples that then turned into a tango. Dani moved with the strength and grace of an ultimate athlete. My heart swelled with pride at their performance.

Eventually, more acts came on, continuing the story when Dani exited the stage and came back with the musicians. The crowd hollered as they lowered into the middle splits, playing their flute and balancing between their two foot loops in their straps.

It was a masterpiece of aerial and circus arts along with singing, dancing, and music. The crowd ate it up, and we clapped viciously every time Dani was on stage.

The evening ended with a standing ovation, and they all came out on stage, smiling and bowing as people whistled. Flowers were thrown on stage, and the clapping roared on. Tears stung my eyes as I watched Dani soak in the praise with a small smile on their lips. I wondered what they were thinking right now?

"Fuck, that was incredible!" Logan said, fanning herself.

"Hot and bothered, are you?" Bex teased.

"It was like straight-up sex on stage, honestly. The tension was delicious," Aven commented, then raked her eyes down Bex's form.

"We should do something like that," Ozzie teased Jess and licked her lips.

"Deal." She winked, and I said nothing as we filtered into the lobby to look for Dani. I wanted to feel my partner's body against mine and tell them they were the most amazing, spectacular human being I had ever seen. Pushing through the crowd, I scanned quickly looking for them, an urgency filling my bones the longer I couldn't find them. Finally, my eyes found them, and it was a punch to the gut how stunning they were.

They stood with admiring fans around them, still donning their costume. The fabric crisscrossed across their arms, legs, and abdomen, making my stomach flutter. Little cutouts of their skin showed through, and I had the urge to trace every single one with my fingers, then with my tongue. They smiled at someone who handed them a bouquet of flowers. Who was that person? An adoring friend who had a secret crush?

GET IT TOGETHER, MYLA.

It seemed like there were endless amounts of people between us—too many people to wade through. My head swam the longer I looked at them, and I swayed a little side to side as tears built in my eyes once again. I really did love them. So much.

The others laughed and joked around me, but it was like time had stopped when I looked at them. I missed them so freaking much.

"Myla," Logan said, and Dani's eyes lit up at the sound of my name. They seemed a bit confused as they narrowed their eyes, looking around before our gazes clashed. It was like all the oxygen in the room was sucked out. Their mouth dropped open as the person next to them kept speaking. My body had its own agenda, because I pushed through the crowd of people, way too aggressively for the average person, to meet them. My steps got quicker the closer we got, and then I rushed them, throwing myself at them and wrapping my arms around their neck and inhaling their scent.

They felt like home.

"Myla!" Dani said, clinging to my back as I nearly sobbed, the ache in my chest easing after weeks of pain.

"Hi," I squealed as they pulled back, and their hands were cupping my face like they couldn't believe I was there. Then everyone else disappeared as their lips slammed against mine. Every worry I'd had about them moving on from me and loving life in Vegas more than our life together vanished with the feeling of their lips on mine.

"Woooo!" Aven hollered, and we stepped back as Dani excused themself from the people around them, who looked at them lovingly.

"What are you all doing here?" Dani looked lighter as they hugged everyone around us as some tension leaked out of their shoulders.

"God, you are a star." Bex beamed at them, and Dani nearly blushed.

"Thank you for coming. I'm speechless. I had no idea!" Dani interlaced their fingers with mine, and my heart soared.

"That was sexy. Truly, you're the hottest, I don't even know what to say." Logan brought over a glass of champagne for them. They accepted it and took a long sip.

"We're only here for the night but wanted to come and cheer you on," Ozzie said, our little circle encompassing Dani.

"Thank you." Their eyes got misty.

"Okay, but if you cry, *I'm* going to cry." Jess patted her cheeks.

"No tears right now. Let me go grab my stuff and do a little cooldown. Please, for the love of god, I would love to leave the overstimulation of this crowd and go somewhere less loud." Dani took a long blink.

"Mission accepted. We will find a place to chill." Aven pulled the group toward the exit. Dani tugged me with them toward backstage.

"You're amazing. Truly the most spectacular performer I've ever seen." I meant it. They had a way of capturing everyone's eyes and hearts when they were on stage.

"I've missed you." Dani pulled me toward a hallway and pushed me against the closet wall, tangling their hands in my hair as I sighed, pressing my lips to theirs. Heat erupted in my belly as we pawed at one another. I heard a noise and pushed Dani away playfully.

A woman came around the corner and beamed at Dani.

"Dani! Oh my gosh, I was wondering where you sneaked off to," she said, looking between the two of us.

"Hi, Katie. This is Myla, my partner. She surprised me by coming tonight." My belly did a funny thing at Dani claiming me as theirs.

"How lovely. I'll give you another thing to celebrate tonight." Katie clapped her hands together. "I just talked with the donors I mentioned earlier, and you sealed the deal, Dani. They want you full time in Vegas for the next three years! How amazing is that? We can talk about details later, but this is a huge deal. They are willing to pay a lot to have you stay here." She winked, and my mouth went dry. "You have an incredibly talented partner, Myla. Enjoy your evening, and I'll talk with you later!" She breezed by, and Dani's eyes were round. They hadn't said anything to the offer, but obviously they'd had a conversation prior.

"Congrats, Dani. That's amazing," I whispered, and they looked at me helplessly.

"Myla, that's not what it looks like," Dani said in a hushed tone.

"You don't have to explain anything." I turned away, tears leaking from my eyes. "I'm going to go find the others. Take your time. You're brilliant, Dani, and it's amazing people are recognizing it." Like a coward, I fled. My heart had ballooned from excitement, lust, and happiness mere moments ago to then being popped by what should have been amazing news. Why was I making this about me?

Geez, I was a horrible partner. I rushed away from Dani.

"Myla, wait!" Dani called out, but I sprinted back out into the crowd, barely able to catch my breath as tears streamed down my eyes. I headed to the closest bathroom. I couldn't help but think Dani was like a beautiful bird who needed to be free, and I only seemed to be caging them in.

TWENTY-EIGHT
DANI

Myla completely ignored the conversation that had happened with Katie the whole evening. She pasted a smile on her face that I had a hard time unraveling. I tried several times to bring it up, even with the others around, but she rapidly changed the subject.

I knew how the conversation must have looked to her. Katie acted like my acceptance was a sure thing. For most performers, it would be a no-brainer. A contract that long and with what I assumed would be a hefty paycheck was a dream come true. There probably weren't many people who would turn it down.

However, I had spent a lot of my life doing things for other people and being someone I wasn't for the comfort of others. I wasn't interested in doing that anymore. If she would just give me a chance to talk to her, then I could clear all of this up. My brain couldn't even fathom being in Vegas for the next three years. I wanted to make art that was mine and with the people I loved, not what would just sell tickets.

"Just a few more weeks, and then you'll be back with us," Logan said excitedly. Myla's face faltered just the tiniest bit.

The cracks in her mask were starting to show, and all I desired was to tell her it was going to be fine. We were going to be fine. I was choosing what I wanted, and that was her and my Cirque Callisto family.

"Yeah, I really can't wait." I looked right at Myla when I said it. Her eyes began to water, and it was like a punch to my gut. Damnit.

"Are you okay?" Jess asked Myla, and Myla swiped at her eyes.

"Yeah, this is just making my eyes water." She motioned to her food. "Super spicy." She sniffled, and Ozzie raised one eyebrow at her. Everyone could see she was distressed.

"Are a lot of the other performers Vegas residents, or are they coming and going?" Bex asked as he sipped his cocktail.

"It's a mix of both. I think a lot of people who are not from here are looking for a residency, but some are just here for the season," I replied.

"I mean, a residency here would be amazing." Myla tried to sound cheerful, but her voice felt flat.

No, no, no.

"If that's what you want, then sure. But Vegas isn't everyone's scene." Aven sat back and crossed her arms.

"Agreed. It's not mine." My eyes drilled into Myla's, and a look of confusion crossed her features. If she wouldn't have the conversation directly with me, then I would find a way to make her understand, whether she was ready to hear it or not.

"You seem genuinely at home here." Myla's voice took on a weird edge, and Logan looked between the two of us. The whole table sat in silence as everyone's eyes bounced between us. A tear slipped down Myla's cheek.

"Something has happened. Do you want us to leave?" Logan's gaze continued to volley across the table.

"No, you don't have to leave." Myla was deflecting the conversation, and I wanted to scream at the top of my lungs.

"Myla, we can do this in private, or we can do this in front of everyone. You've been ignoring me all night and haven't let me even say anything about what Katie said," I begged. I wanted to end this misery for her, and for myself.

Myla looked like she was ready to bolt. She tried to stand up abruptly as more tears leaked from her wide eyes. Bex and Ozzie grabbed her and shoved her ass back in her seat as she squirmed and furrowed her brows.

"Myla, stop being avoidant and listen to Dani, for Christ's sake. Everyone will know about this anyway," Ozzie said, and Bex snorted. Myla looked crestfallen.

"What is this, a freaking ambush?" Myla's voice was pitched high, and more tears rolled down her cheeks.

"No, no! I just wanted to tell you I'm not taking Katie's offer!" I said seriously. Everyone around us swiveled their eyes to Myla, whose jaw dropped open. She looked like she didn't believe me.

"You have to take the offer," Myla said quietly.

"No, I don't. I don't want to. I don't want what Vegas has to offer." As the words came out of my mouth, I knew they were my truth.

"You can't turn down something like this for me." Myla's lip quivered, like it pained her to say the words that tumbled out of her mouth.

"Myla, I love you so fucking much, and the reason I'm not taking the offer is because of a million different reasons..."

Everyone took a sharp inhale of breath, and I looked right at her.

"Cirque Callisto"—I gestured to our friends around us— "is my home. I have never had a place that felt explicitly mine. That I yearned to settle into. Does part of that have to do with you? Absolutely, but part of it is because I don't want to break my body and be so busy I have no time for anything else. Vegas is an intensity I'm not interested in. The money is great, but it's way more important for me to be somewhere I feel loved, supported, and cared for. You are a part of that, as is everyone else. I want to make art that doesn't have to fit into one particular mold. I love performing, and I don't need thousands of people and thousands of dollars to be the only reasons I do it."

"Dani." Myla's tears flooded from her eyes.

"I'm tired of going from place to place looking for something that makes me feel seen. You all do that. Vegas absolutely does not. And if that just so happens to be where the love of my life is, then it sounds like a pretty fucking easy decision to me." I breathed heavily, my chest feeling a million times lighter. This decision was mine, and it was right. I would not be pressured into something I no longer wanted to do, not by money or fame or anything else.

"You love me?" Myla bit her lip and shuddered.

"Of course I love you. I need you to trust my ability to make these decisions for myself and accept whatever consequences I might face because of them. This has been amazing, but it isn't what I want the rest of my life to be like," I said gently.

"Okay," she whispered.

"And it's fine if you don't love me yet—I can be patient and wait—but you just need to know that's how I feel," I said. I would wait years to hear the words from her mouth. I knew where my heart was, and I only hoped one day she would feel the same.

Myla stood up and flung herself onto my lap.

"I love you, Dani. So much. If this is what you wanted for your career, I would have stood behind it. I just didn't want you to give up something for me. I would never forgive myself. But I trust you, and I love you with my whole heart." Then she pressed her lips to mine, and I tangled my hands into her purple hair, feeling the heat of her body against mine. It was like everything felt clear and bright again.

Our little table erupted in applause.

"Well if that wasn't the most romantic thing I have ever bore witness to..." Logan sniffled.

Ozzie and Jess clung to one another. "Aw, look at Cirque Callisto bringing love to the air," Jess exclaimed.

"Let's not forget that you were a little asshat about me staying here for similar reasons too." Ozzie pinched Jess's side, and Jess pinched her right back.

"Let's get a round of champagne!" Aven announced.

The waiter came around and brought us a bottle. My heart felt lighter and freer than it had for weeks.

"To love!" Bex toasted, and looked right at Aven, who pointedly looked the other way. God, those two were a storm waiting to happen.

"To love!" we all echoed back. Myla still sat on my lap, and I rubbed circles into her back.

"Katie told me right before the show about the deal and told me not to focus on it until she knew for sure it would go through. Her telling me with you there was the first I knew that it was genuinely real. I hadn't yet gotten a chance to tell her I appreciated it, but it wasn't for me," I said quietly, wanting to run my tongue along her neck and nuzzle into her skin.

Myla nodded. "I understand now. I'm sorry for jumping to conclusions." She tugged on her hair and smiled sheepishly.

"I know. But I'm excited to come back to you and our people." I snuggled my face into her hair and inhaled the scent that was all Myla.

"Can I stay with you tonight?" she asked.

"Yes, please."

"Ew, get a room," Aven said teasingly.

"Don't worry, we got one." I winked, and they all laughed.

The rest of the evening was full of love and laughter from the people I held most dear to my heart. It ended with Myla in my bed, coming on my mouth. Then my fingers. Then a fun new strap-on.

"Dani," she panted as I made her writhe with pleasure.

"Say it again, Myla." I curled my fingers inside her as her back arched off my bed and her pretty nipples pressed to the sky.

"I love you, I love you, I love you," she practically screamed.

"There's a good girl," I purred. We spent the rest of the night showing one another how much we truly meant it, and it was the best night of my life.

———

The rest of my time in Vegas zipped by after Myla and the others left. Soaren came and saw my last show. Katie took it better than I'd thought when I told her I had to turn down the offer.

"I get it. A Vegas residency is not for everyone. You should be really proud of the performer you are, Dani. You're magnificent, and anytime you want more work, let me know. You're a star." She hugged me, and I felt effervescent.

It took a few days to load out and close down the show with the cast parties and final touches that happened at the end of such a large production. But when it was finally over, I was able to breathe fully again.

It took all my power to be patient as I wrapped up my time here. Myla and I got to talk more now that we weren't holding one another at arm's length.

"We have our performance together, you know, in just a

few short weeks," Myla said on the phone. We still had to prepare and practice for our set together.

"I know. I can't wait to be with you on stage," I commented, and meant it. Myla made everything feel magical, and I loved her for it.

"Hurry your butt home, and then we can get to it," she teased.

"I'm literally sitting at the airport doing just that."

This was it. My time in Vegas had come to an end, and I was grateful for it. Soaren had promised to come see Myla's and my performance and bring Lily since it was definitely kid-friendly compared to some of the other things I did.

"Looks like we're boarding," I said as I stood up with my things.

"Okay, I love you, Dani. Be safe. I'll see you in a few hours," Myla replied.

"I love you too, Myla. See you soon." And I hung up. My heart was so full, and I was ready to start our lives together. Myla was my happily-ever-after, and I couldn't wait to see where life would take us.

EPILOGUE
MYLA

Tonight was the night I got to perform with the love of my life, and I couldn't be more nervous about it. All I wanted was to take a week-long vacation with Dani and have them all to myself.

After everything we had been through, and everything I had been through in the past year, I was ready for some ease.

"How are you feeling about tonight?" Logan asked as I began my methodical process of doing my makeup and hair for the performance.

"Great. I can't wait to do this and then take a break now that Dani is here. We're together. And everything feels like it's right again."

"I'm glad everything worked out the way it did. You two are made for one another." Logan gave me a squeeze from behind, a little sadness in her eyes.

"Are you okay, Lo?" I turned to face her, and she fiddled with some pink strands of her hair. My heart was happy with where my own life had taken me, but I had never asked if Logan was happy with hers. She was a formidable force with friends that loved her, but sometimes her work was lonely. We wanted to help, but she kept things close to her heart.

"Yes, I'm happy for you all, yet it's like everyone is coupled off except me. I'm not really a relationship girl, but I can't help but maybe feel a little jealous now that it feels like everyone has someone but me, you know?" She winced like the admission pained her.

Logan wasn't normally vulnerable about this type of stuff. She was an "I don't need a man" type of person, but I could see this was weighing heavily on her.

"I understand that. You can be simultaneously happy for us and sad for you. Those emotions can happen at the same time, you know." I stood up and wrapped my arms around her. Any partner would be lucky to have her, but I knew she had built up walls of protection for herself. We all had our reasons, and Logan's was a damn good one.

"You all are just disgustingly adorable. I cannot fucking stand it, you motherfuckers." She sniffled and wiped at her eyes, her confident mask sliding back into place, like this moment had never happened. She placed a wide smile on her face and exhaled loudly.

"That's a lot of fucks thrown in there." I laughed, and she did too.

She waved her hand around her face. "But I'll be fine. You all know I'm high maintenance in the best way, and I won't settle for anyone who can't keep up with that. The universe has dealt me a shitty hand before, and I will be damned if I let something like that happen again."

Dani walked in at that moment, beaming at me, and my heart skipped a beat.

"Lo, are you alright?" Dani looked concerned as they scanned Logan's face. Her smile slipped just a little before it was right back in place again.

"Yes. I'll be fine. Nothing to worry about here. I'll see you two out there." She sniffled and exited the green room. The moment of vulnerability fizzled out as her confident stride and armor slid back into place.

"Is she really going to be okay? Logan hardly ever cries." Dani didn't look convinced, and neither was I. But she would talk to us when she was ready. I just hoped she would let us help before the weight crushed her.

"She's just feeling a little emotionally vulnerable right now, but I think she will be alright," I said, hoping the words I was saying were true.

Dani nodded and came over to me, gently cupping my jaw.

"You look lovely," they purred, and heat pooled between my thighs.

"I'm only halfway through all my prep." I giggled, feeling precious and beautiful under their gaze.

"And it's still hot." Dani pulled my mouth to theirs, and we got lost in each other's lips for a few moments before I pulled away. It felt good to be together again and performing with them. I had so many ideas of what we could do together, on and off the stage.

"I do need to finish this, though, and you need to get ready too!" I said, slapping them on their butt.

"Fine, fine. I'll do as you say." They complied, and we both went to work on getting ready for the event.

Our outfits were complements of one another: I wore a black sequined leotard with one arm and leg fully covered and the other arm and leg exposed, and Dani wore a version of a tuxedo with a cinched black vest and flared dress pants.

"We're hot." I slinked up behind them and squeezed around their waist. We looked like a perfect pair together.

"Yeah we are." They turned and kissed my cheek.

"Ready to do this?" Butterflies fluttered in my belly. I felt like a bottle of bubbling champagne, all giddy and fizzling with joy.

I nodded, and they grabbed their instrument. We walked hand in hand out of the room, smiling at everyone who was invited to the event, and making our way to the small stage, where Logan was with the rest of our friends. Jess and Ozzie were wrapped around each other, laughing and drinking champagne, while Bex and Aven were close, but not too close.

"I wonder what is actually going on between those two," I commented. Whenever they had it out, it would be with fireworks—good or bad, I still wasn't sure.

"They'll figure it out." Dani shrugged.

Logan stood talking animatedly with some food in her hands until she spotted us.

"You ready?" she asked.

We nodded as the announcer took the stage, introducing us and what we would be doing tonight for the party. There was applause as we made our way to take the stage.

Dani nodded at me and started their song. The notes floated around, and I took a deep breath, grabbing my fabric and moving around the stage with flares and flicks of the glossy, deep-red silks.

Then I began to climb. Splits and spins and drops were timed perfectly to the music, and I got lost in the strength and concentration of my act, with Dani's notes wrapping around me for support.

The first song ended with me climbing all the way to the top and dropping a foot from the floor, where the audience cheered and hollered.

"Yes, Myla!" Bex screamed, and I beamed, artfully untangling myself and taking a bow with Dani. We went right into our next song. The next few weren't quite as dramatic. The guests were served drinks and dinner, decidedly ignoring us when food and booze arrived. I was breathless by the time I was done, and Dani continued to play several more songs, even after I left for my break.

"That was fabulous, Myla. My contact here already asked about having us back and said there were a few other people interested in hiring us based on your and Dani's performance alone," Logan praised.

"I always think silks are beautiful when you do it, then I get up there and I hate the fabric with a passion," Jess said, popping a grape into her mouth, and I laughed.

"Good thing you don't need to be up there then." I pushed her shoulder playfully.

Dani joined us shortly after they had put away their instrument and slid next to me as guests continued to come up and comment on our performance. My heart was full.

"Dani!" A man who looked deceptively similar to Dani came up with a small girl in his arms.

"Soaren! Lily!" Dani collided with them in a big hug. This was Dani's brother and niece. I could see how much love and care they had for them.

"You must be Myla." Soaren set Lily down, and Dani bent down to talk with her as she giggled.

"I am. It's nice to meet you, Soaren." He engulfed me in a hug, and I squeezed him back, the sudden urge to cry happy tears pricking the backs of my eyes.

"You two were magical out there. Thank you for allowing us to join today." Soaren stepped back as Lily looped her hand in Dani's.

"You look like a Disney princess," Lily said, smiling at me.

"Thank you, Lily. It's nice to meet you."

"Are you Dani's partner?" Lily asked, looking between the two of us.

"I am," I said, impressed by her use of the word "partner." People liked to act like kids wouldn't understand, but they were the most understanding of us all.

"She's pretty." Lily looked at Dani, who nodded in agreement.

"Aren't you two adorable?" Logan sidled up next to us, and looked at Lily and Soaren.

"Logan, Soaren and Lily. Lily and Soaren, Logan." Dani made the introductions.

"Daddy! I want colored hair like them." Lily looked wide-eyed at Logan's pink hair and my purple.

"Maybe we can play with spray-on hair paint?" Soaren asked.

"Okay!" She clapped excitedly, and we all laughed.

For the rest of the evening, we did a few more sets and ended with Dani accompanying me on the silks. We tangled in the fabric with one another and held each other close as the final notes of our song ended. It got a standing ovation from nearly everyone in the room.

The evening ended with us spending time with Soaren and Lily. They were absolutely delightful, and it was good to see Dani at ease with the people they loved. They were staying with us, since we'd turned one of the bedrooms into a guest room. Finally, I'd said goodbye to my old bed. We'd decided Dani's bed was where the two of us would sleep and do many other things together.

"Thank you for letting them stay at the house," Dani said as we snuggled into each other at the end of the long performance evening.

"Of course. This is your home too, and they're your people. I love that they're here. Thanks for letting me meet your family." I booped Dani on their nose, and they smirked.

"Where do we go from here?" Dani asked, our breaths mingling together.

"What do you mean?"

"I mean, now that we're settled in, what's next, Myla?" Dani asked.

"How about a life of ease and love and fun?" I shot back.

"And sex?" they added.

"Oh, lots of sex. In fact, I think we can start with that one now," I said smoothly as I slid my hands along their sides, and they sighed into me. Their skin felt warm underneath my touch, and I wanted to get lost in all the beautiful sounds of their pleasure.

"Myla..." Dani breathed, and I slid underneath the sheets, trailing kisses along their torso and hip bones. They arched their back and sighed.

"Tell me what you want, Dani," I said against their soft skin.

"Your mouth." They fisted the sheets underneath us as I dipped my tongue into their soft, wet center.

"Please make me come, Myla," they moaned.

"Your wish is my command." I settled between their legs and went to work licking and lapping them, showing them exactly what it would be like to be mine forever.

They groaned in pleasure, moaning my name as I whispered "I love you" against their skin and decided if this was how I was going to spend the rest of my life, I would die a happy woman.

THE END

ACKNOWLEDGMENTS

There are always so many people who make publishing a book possible.

Thank you, Rose, my friend and editor, for helping this book become the best version of itself.

Thank you, Emily, for answering me in my time of need and making this book sparkle.

Thank you, Madeline, for being willing to do whatever it took to get this book out when I reached out at the last minute.

Thank you, Amanda, for making the covers for this entire series. Each one is spectacular in its own way, and I love each of them deeply.

Thank you to my parents, who absolutely champion me as an artist and creative every single time.

Thank you to my alphas, betas, and all the readers in between who offered advice, corrections, or a word of encouragement before this book became a reality.

Thank you, especially, to my own circus. There are so many of you who make my days and weeks joyous. I don't know what I would do without you all. Thank you for hollering about my queer, smutty circus books louder than anyone else.

Thank you to every single person on Bookthreads, Bookstagram, and Booktok who interacts with my constant shouting into the void and sharing your love for my projects on your social media and with your friends. I would not be able to do this without you all.

And thank you to all my readers. Thank you for joining me on this circus journey. I hope you stay awhile.

AUTHOR'S NOTE

I can't believe we are already at book two of the Cirque Callisto Series! Each book has a lot of my own experience as a circus professional, but please keep in mind that things have been dramatized and exaggerated for the purpose of writing this book in different ways.

However, if you're looking to have a lot of fun, I would highly recommend checking out your local circus center, as I do think we find a lot of joy doing what we do.

Myla's queer experience heavily reflects my own, but please know everyone's experience with their queer identity is unique and valid. I was with a man for a long time and never thought about my sexuality until I left and realized I was queer. You will often see me use bisexual, queer, and pansexual to describe my characters and myself, because my identity is fluid and ever changing. It depends on who I am talking to, safety, level of understanding of queer identities, as well as what feels most authentic to me. I understand that is not everyone's view or experience with queer identities, but that is what mine looks like presently.

Similarly to Dani's experience, being nonbinary looks

different for every person, and there is no right way—only your way. Being queer is beautiful and unique to each individual. My goal is to celebrate that in these stories and show that finding love exactly as you are is a wonderful and magical thing.

Especially in our current political climate, I encourage you to lead with love, empathy, and support of those around you. LGBTQIA2S+ people will always exist and persist. Please continue to champion our voices and keep us safe. Together as a community, we will not stop fighting.

Reviews

If you want to share your thoughts and feelings about *Unexpected Attachments*, please share your review on Amazon and Goodreads. Reviews are really helpful for independent authors and truly help them find their audience. Additionally, feel free to send an email to info@madisonnicolebooks.com. I welcome all feedback and would love to hear from you!

Social Media

If you would like to stay updated on all the new book things, you can see my shenanigans here:

TikTok | Instagram | Threads
@madisonnicolebooks

Or get signed copies here:

Website: www.madisonnicolebooks.com

About the Author

Madison Nicole is a 29-year-old queer author who currently lives in Kansas City, where she teaches dance, fitness, and circus arts. You can catch Madi playing video games, reading dark romance books, and juggling when she is not writing. She is excited to continue to explore her writing career and bring more stories your way!

ALSO BY MADISON NICOLE
AVAILABLE ON KU

Cirque Callisto Series
Tangled Encounters

The Immortality Trials Trilogy
The Immortality Trials

Standalones
Deathwalker, a sapphic fantasy romance
Not Queer Enough, a queer contemporary romance

A SNEAK PEAK INTO
DEATHWALKER...

CHAPTER 1

"How many people do you think actually use their college degree?" I asked, taking a sip of my coffee. I turned to my best friend, Mara, expectantly. We were lounging on the large sectional in our apartment, spending a lazy Saturday morning watching a Lord of the Rings movie marathon on TV.

"I mean...I don't know. People change their minds about what they want to do all the time. Most degrees are relatively versatile, you know," she said, shrugging her dark brown shoulders. Her hazel eyes were still slightly sleep-deprived, considering she'd been out a lot of the night drinking with her new boy toy.

"Thinking of switching your job again?" she asked, taking a long sip from her coffee mug.

I let out a loud sigh, "I mean, maybe...."

I graduated college almost four years ago and basically get a new job every year. I am restless as hell. The pressure of having my shit figured out often works its way up my spine into my chest where it slowly suffocates me. It feels like my heart's running marathons while my body's completely immobilized. It seems to be getting worse as of late, which probably means I need to schedule an appointment with my therapist. Other people are absolutely fine not loving their jobs, without freaking out and quitting after a year. So why do I flee every job like I've committed some heinous crime in the office break room? Am I the weird one or is it everyone else? Sometimes, I just feel defective.

"Talk to me, Lincoln," Mara said, pulling her full attention to me and giving me a soft smile as she fiddled with her long dark braids.

"I just don't understand why I can't be satisfied with anything. I got a business degree to have options, you know? And every job I've tried, I feel like something goes wrong. I'm drowning! Why can't I just be a normal fucking human being who works their miserable life away and gets drunk on the weekend and stays busy to cope?" I huffed out the words, clenching my hands in the blanket wrapped around me. I ground my teeth together and closed my eyes for a minute to re-collect my thoughts.

"Linc, it's okay that you don't have things figured out. We are literally only twenty-five...," she said, reaching over and giving my hand a squeeze. Mara knows the good, bad, and ugly about me. We have been inseparable since we were young and she is very familiar with my ongoing existential crisis.

"Have you talked to Isaac about it? I mean, since you guys are engaged now, maybe he'll help fund an *Eat, Pray, Love* moment for you," she said winking, tucking her feet underneath her and snuggling deeper into the couch.

"Yeah, he said he would support whatever I do," I said, smiling slightly.

"See, problem solved," she said playfully, pushing my shoulder.

I looked down at the diamond on my hand and sighed. It's

a pretty spectacular ring since I designed it myself: a rose gold band with a large emerald cut diamond, and small black stones on the side. No need to make him play guessing games about what I wanted. I simply created it myself.

Issac proposed just two months ago, and we are already in the throes of wedding planning. It almost freaks me out more than my job. I feel like a mess, financially and emotionally. It didn't seem like the best way to start a marriage, but there would never be a perfect time. "Perfect" just didn't exist, and we both fully accepted one another for who we are.

Isaac has his shit together as a mechanical engineer who makes good money and has a *regular* job. I'm the one going wild trying to find something that matches the constant restlessness inside my body. And he knows all this. We're incredibly transparent and honest about our feelings. But sometimes it's hard for me to rely on other people. I want to be a strong, independent woman who doesn't need *no man*. Even though I want to be with Isaac, I just don't want to *need* him.

Isaac and I have been dating on and off again for almost ten years. We met when we were in high school and fell in love hard and fast. We had some ups and downs, and periods of finding ourselves where we didn't speak for a couple of years. But for the most part, he just got me in a way no one else did. I always thought of him even when we weren't technically together.

I love him with my whole freaking heart and I'm ready for that part of my life to fall into place, even though it's scary. At least one part of my life will be grounded, and everything's easier with someone constant and reliable by my side. I had talked to him about it, to which he said he would financially support us as I tried to navigate what the hell I wanted to do. Right now, I'm working for several companies doing freelance social media marketing, and it's fine. However, I'm exhausted and bored with it. I need something else, some other purpose to drive me.

I tried corporate marketing and that sucked balls, not to mention my manager was actually the spawn of Satan herself. Then I tried event planning for a local company and found out that working every single weekend *also* sucked some major balls. After that, I tried working at a coffee shop but the money really wasn't good enough, and there was no way in hell I was living with my parents, so I started running businesses' social media pages. There was a lot of Googling and YouTubing involved on how to make the best social media decisions, but part of that came with the job. It was easy work compared to being emotionally spat on every day, but it wasn't fulfilling in the way I needed it to be.

"You love your job, though. You make nice money AND you have a good work-life balance," I said, staring at Mara accusingly, like she had the answer I was desperately looking for and she was just refusing to share. "What's the secret, my precious?"

"Ew, please keep your Gollum references to yourself. There is no secret, babe. I just found it. It's not like I knew being a pharmacist was going to be exactly what I wanted to do. Plus, you found a long-term committed relationship first so, we are one for one here on the expectations society puts on twenty-five-year-olds, okay? I mean, neither of us has a house or children so we're a little behind on a few other things, but hey, we can't do it all," she said, laughing loudly at her own joke and downing her coffee.

"Yeah, except a man can't make you feel purposeful and fulfilled in your own life, no matter what Disney promised us when we were younger," I mumbled. "Don't even speak to me about the other things you mentioned either. I can only handle one thing at a time," I said, throwing my head back to stare at the ceiling.

"You and me both," Mara chuckled.

I didn't like feeling lost. I was the one who normally had my shit together. I was the one with the five-year plan my entire life until I graduated college. Then I realized that I didn't have a single clue what I was supposed to do for the rest of my life. I felt like I was having a midlife crisis *all the time* and it was getting really old, *really* fast.

"Linc, you'll figure it out. Give yourself some grace and empathy here. You don't have to have it together all the time," she said, getting up and moving towards the kitchen.

"Tell that to my steady stream of anxiety," I said. I set my coffee aside and lay down on the couch, hoping it would just swallow me whole. My phone buzzed on the wooden coffee table, and Issac's name popped up. Smiling, I reached for it.

> **Isaac: Hey babe! I want to talk to you about something. Can we grab dinner at your place tonight? I'll bring pad thai.**

I don't know why but whenever someone says they want to talk to me about something, my stomach immediately drops to my ass. But this is Isaac. We tell each other everything. He's my fiancé and my best friend.

> **Me: Okay! Is it bad? Should I be scared? ;)**

His reply came a few seconds later.

> **Isaac: Haha not necessarily! I'll be there around 6:30pm.**

Okayyy, weird.

Me: Cool, sounds good. I love you!

Isaac: Love you too.

"Hey! Isaac and I are talking about something important tonight. Could we have the apartment to ourselves?" I said, peeking over the back of the couch to stare into our kitchen, where Mara was rubbing her eyes and refilling her mug.

"Oooh, sounds serious. Yeah, I think I'm going to see that guy again tonight! Is it wedding-related? You know, as your best friend and maid of honor, I should be privy to this shit," she said, shuffling around, sipping on her third cup of coffee.

"Yeah, he's being kinda vague about it, but maybe? Who knows? Want to go to a yoga class, and then we can both get ready for our hot dates?" I said, grabbing my phone again to look at the time.

"Yesss! I need to release some of this liquor," Mara said, closing her eyes and taking a deep breath.

"Cool. I just need to chill the fuck out," I said standing up and stretching my legs. I headed toward my room and sighed, wondering what Isaac wanted to talk about.

———

"Hi," I said, snatching up the food from Isaac's hands and leaning in to plant a kiss on his cheek. Isaac's such a hottie. He's tall, dark, and handsome down to a tee. He smiled, flashing his perfectly straight teeth, but it didn't reach his eyes. "You seem nervous," I said. "Everything okay?"

He swallowed and nodded, "Of course." He stepped inside and shut the door behind him. He was wearing a dark red sweater that complemented his tanned skin. His dark hair had little snowflakes in it, and I resisted the urge to brush them away. He wore black jeans that hugged his muscular thighs and brown boots that were covered in slush.

My heart squeezed at the sight of him. I wanted to wrap my hands around his broad shoulders and drag him to bed, but also...food. I really wanted this delicious pad thai, and I was starting to get nervous about whatever he wanted to talk about. With the takeout containers in hand, I headed over to the couch, ready to dig into the noodles. Isaac sat on the other side of the couch with a tall spine and didn't reach for the container I had set out for him.

"Linc," he started as I put a whole forkful of the delicious-smelling noodles in my mouth. "I don't want to get married."

I started choking on my food and coughing as my eyes bugged out of my head.

Did I seriously just hear that right?

What. The. Hell!

"Oh my god, are you okay?" Isaac asked, suddenly worried and frantically getting water as I recovered from nearly being choked to death by our dinner.

I nodded my head and took a huge swig from the glass in front of me. I just stared at him, waiting for him to say he was kidding, that I was getting Punk'd. Do people still say that? Or do that?

He said the conversation wasn't bad. I was confused at how any of what just came out of his mouth wasn't considered "bad." Was this a joke? It had to be a joke. But who would make a joke about something like that? Why would Isaac make a joke about that? My thoughts raced through my head, and anxiety started to wrap its way around my throat. A pit I didn't know existed in my stomach started to open up with no bottom in sight. The ability to speak seemed to have left my body.

"Did you hear what I said?" Isaac's dark brown eyes scanned my face, and he started chewing his bottom lip.

Silence hung in the air, and I suddenly had no desire to eat anything at all.

"This is what you wanted to talk about...," I said slowly. My stomach turned into knots, and my whole body tensed up like I was getting ready to jump out of a fucking plane. He nodded and opened his mouth to start again, then closed it, running his hands through his dark hair and casting his eyes down.

"What the fuck?!" I was finally able to find words for what was happening inside me. Anger and hurt swelled in my belly from the depths of someplace I didn't even know existed. Isaac's face paled and he took that opportunity to start babbling like a complete and utter idiot.

"I just don't think I'm ready for this. I want us to be together, but what if we just put a pause on the wedding, you know? Like, I don't even know if I believe in marriage. I've never known a happily married couple, and my parents were shit at it. My dad's been married three times now. Like, what does marriage even mean?"

I blinked at him stupidly, not knowing how to respond to anything that was coming out of his mouth. His gaze kept bouncing around the room like he could barely stand to look at me.

"And I just feel like I need to figure some stuff out on my own, and I still want to be together. I just don't want the wedding or marriage part. I've been feeling this way for a while, and I just can't do it anymore with the impending wedding. I am freaking out, and we've been kind of distant and disconnected which definitely means we shouldn't be getting married...." He continued to prattle on with a number of reasons and excuses to justify himself, and I felt like time was standing still.

I wanted to scream. To cry. To fling this goddamn pad thai at the wall. But I sat still, letting him talk himself to death until finally, he trailed off. His eyes finally found mine, and he looked at me expectantly.

"Why did you propose then?" I said, trying to find the right questions to ask and make sense of the literal bomb that just went off in my life. I scrambled to grab at anything that made sense. My thoughts and feelings were fractured like broken glass and every time I tried to pick up a piece, it sliced straight into my heart.

"You wanted me to," he said, like that was a full, complete thought and not some utter bullshit, like I had forced him into a proposal. As if he hadn't been an active participant in the whole thing.

Tears stung the backs of my eyes and I felt like I couldn't get enough oxygen to my brain. My hands started to shake with rage and my whole body felt ready to combust in a million little pieces.

"We talked about this, *together*," I said, my voice rising in a high-pitched tone. "We talked about each of our relationships and feelings about marriage and what we wanted from our future together. We agreed, *together*, that marriage and a wedding was our next step. Or did you suddenly forget about those conversations? We agreed *together* that this was the life we were building." Tears had finally come and were pouring down my cheeks from anger, betrayal, and hurt. My heart throbbed, and I felt like I had a sudden case of the stomach flu.

"I just feel like I'm not happy right now. I need to work on myself. I haven't felt happy for a long time," he said, whispering into his takeout container.

"How long?" I said, biting out each word. He didn't address any of what I said earlier, and I was fuming. I wanted answers. I wanted a reason that felt justified. I needed a better "why" than this rambly-ass explanation. I attempted to steady my breathing but I couldn't. My whole body was on fucking fire and my stomach was doing acrobatics.

"Like, a year or so...." He looked at me with tears in his eyes.

I swear to god he has no fucking right to cry right now.

"You didn't tell me for a *year* that you weren't happy? Who the fuck are you?! Were you just saying what I wanted to hear all these months and now, at the fucking finish line, you realize you can't do this anymore?" I screamed as I shook violently.

Remember how I said we were always honest and transparent with one another? Welp, I was royally, painfully, and stupidly wrong.

I let that realization wash over me, that the small white lies he'd told in order to fit in or make others more comfortable extended to our relationship too. I thought I knew the little fibs he told were just his way of coping in social situations, but obviously it was more. Suddenly, I understood that because he didn't know what he wanted or who he was, he had become a chameleon in every situation, including our relationship.

"I just don't know what to do," he said again, his lips trembling.

"So let me get this straight. All of the conversations we had prior to this, you've conveniently forgotten. You've been unhappy for a long time, but I had no way to help you because you didn't tell me *and* you want to stay together but call off the wedding because you suddenly don't believe in the sanctity of marriage? Even though my parents have already invested thousands of dollars into a wedding, and we've told our friends and family? And let me guess, you want me to deal with that bullshit because I *always* deal with our bullshit?" I stood, flinging my hands around as I paced the room.

My fists clenched so tightly that my nails dug in and blood prickled out. I always pick up the mess. I'm the one that always caved and said I was sorry first because I didn't want to fight. How had I not seen that before?

"Lincoln, I still love you. I just can't do all of this right now. Let's just stop the wedding and work through this together," he said, his eyes pleading.

I was completely and utterly rocked by the words coming out of his mouth. Like he was some alien from space.

"We could try couples therapy," I said letting my hopes soar high for a few fleeting moments, as if I could wrangle in the hurt and chaos of the last ten minutes. Then I could return to my normal tumultuous life where the biggest issue I was dealing with was my own personal identity crisis, and not slapping on the baggage of a broken relationship and wedding on top of that.

"I don't want to do that," Isaac screwed up his face like the idea repulsed him. Like I hadn't used therapy myself to cope with my own anxiety and depression. Like he was too goddamned good for it.

"How the hell are we going to move past this, then? You want to keep doing what we're doing to fix this supposed unhappy, disconnected feeling you're having? That apparently you've been lying about for over a year without changing anything? Are you delusional?" I slammed my hands on the coffee table and snarled at him, my chest heaving. "You need to figure this out on your own, without me. Because I will not sit here and let you play pretend with me or my life any longer. We have known each other too fucking long and been together for too many years for you to treat me this way. You said you wanted this. *You* proposed to *me*. Don't act like I forced you into this, you asshole. Get out!" I pushed away from the coffee table and walked to the front door.

"Lincoln please, I don't want to be without you. I love you. I just can't deliver on marriage," he said, standing up and moving towards me.

"Then you shouldn't have said you could. You shouldn't have lied to my face. You should've figured that shit out before you set the expectation. So get out. I'll cancel all the wedding stuff and, honestly, don't fucking call me. Lose my number. Lose everything that I ever gave you in this relationship because I am out. We have done this too many times, broken up and gotten back together, over the years for you to do this to me. I deserve someone who wants to be with me forever." Tears ran down my cheeks and I swiped at them. "I *want* marriage. I've always wanted it and you knew that, yet you played along anyways. Fuck you! Get the fuck out of my house and don't fucking come back!" I ripped the ring off my hand and shoved it in his face.

"Please don't do this. We can still be together." He looked down at the ring helplessly.

My mind was scattered in a million places as I started to realize my picture-perfect relationship had cracks and holes that I had tried to ignore. I'd compromised and made myself less for this. How did I not know better? How did I let this happen?

I don't know who I was more angry at. Isaac or myself? Either way, I couldn't do this with him right now. I needed him to leave and to let me fix what had broken inside of me. How could I have let this happen in the first place? I really needed him to exit and never come back.

"You did this. And no we can't. This is no longer good enough for me. Love isn't enough for me anymore. *You* are no longer enough. Leave. Now." I grabbed his hand and closed it hard over the ring in his palm. I wanted to vomit from the touch. I could barely stand to look at him, let alone maintain any sort of physical contact. I practically kicked him out the door.

"I'm sorry, Lincoln, please," was all I heard as I slammed the door behind him and sunk down into the floor, feeling the weight of the entire world crash into me. I wrapped my arms around my knees, and the tears poured out in waves. My body trembled as my whole future, and world, was flipped upside down.

I mourned the life I had been planning for years.

The relationship I thought I had.

Isaac.

And the girl who allowed herself to be fooled and blinded by dumb, stupid love.